COLDWATER ENDGAME

COLDWATER ENDGAME

A Coldwater Mystery

JAMES A. ROSS

First published by Level Best Books 2024

Author Photo Credit: Taylor Lenci

First edition

ISBN: 978-1-68512-674-2

Cover art by Rebecacovers & Ryan Mahan

This book was professionally typeset on Reedsy.
Find out more at reedsy.com

Father Donald T. Fussner, 1931-2018
Oraculi et amici

"And the sins of the fathers shall be visited upon the children, and upon the children's children, unto the third and to the fourth generation."

—Exodus 34:6-7

Awards for the Coldwater Series

Coldwater Revenge:

- Winner of the 2021 CLUE Award in the Suspense/Thriller Category.
- Finalist for the National Indie Excellence Award: Crime Fiction Category
- Finalist for 2021 CLUE International Book Awards
- First Place Winner of the Firebird Book Award for Legal/Thriller.
- Winner of the American Fiction Award in the Mystery/Suspense: Hard-boiled/Crime Category
- Winner of the 2021 Pencraft Fiction Award in the Thriller-Terrorist Category
- Winner of the Pinnacle Award in the Thriller Category
- Winner of the Maincrest Book Award in the Mystery/Suspense Category
- Runner Up for the Indies Today Award in the Mystery Category

Coldwater Confession:

- Runner Up in the General Fiction category at the New York Book Festival
- Winner of the 2022 NABE Pinnacle Award in the Mystery Category
- 2022 Bookfest Award Winner in the Category Mystery-Murder & Crime
- 2022 Outstanding Creator Award in the Mystery Category, 3rd Place
- 2023 Pacific Book Award Finalist in the Mystery Category
- 2023 Pencraft Award, 2nd Place in the Mystery Category
- Winner of the 2023 Maincrest Media Award in the Category: Mystery

Chapter One

Luke sat alone in a tree stand, silent, nervous, and unmoving. His neck and face were streaked with green camouflage paint and they felt hot and sticky. The worn brown wood of an ancient Browning compound bow that had belonged to Luke's father when he was a boy was too large for Luke's ten-year-old grip. But his shooting hand, attached firmly to the bowstring by a Velcro strap and mechanical release, could launch a lethal arrow at 300 feet per second with only slight pressure from his right index finger. Luke was excited, and for the first time in a long time, he was happy.

Scanning the thorn-filled gully below the tree stand for signs of movement, he sipped a silent breath and reminded himself that his dad was down there somewhere in the thick brush, stalking slowly uphill. Not quite silent, the sound of his father's footsteps and camouflage cloth scraping against brush would push any deer that might be hiding there uphill toward Luke's tree stand. "Don't shoot unless you see horns," were his dad's final instructions. Luke wouldn't. He'd practiced, and he could hit the center of a pie plate at thirty yards nearly every time. But now his hands trembled, and the sound of his breath was loud in his ears. It took him a long time to settle down.

Almost an hour passed before he heard the telltale sound of hard hoof on dry leaf and saw movement behind a dense thicket of thorn bush. A doe and two yearlings appeared in the gully below the tree stand, dropping their heads to feed on fallen acorns. Luke's heart whirred like a cake mixer. The wood under his hand felt moist.

Opening the hand to admit dry air was a rookie mistake. Three pairs of soft brown eyes turned toward the movement. Then, like a choreographed dance, three snow-white tails lifted high in graceful bounds and disappeared into the thick cover. Luke let out a slow, controlled breath. *Wow!*

For the next few minutes, thoughts and feelings combined and recombined as if passing through a brass kaleidoscope: red and ocher fall woods, dappled deer, and the happiness he felt at being back in Coldwater. Living with Grandma and Grandpa in Canada had been hard. They were nice people. But their house was small, and Grandpa was too often grumpy. Mom had been quiet most of the time they were there. She still was. Dad seemed okay now. He didn't get angry with Luke or his sisters very often, or even with Mom anymore. Luke was happy to be back at his old school with his old friends and to be out in the woods with his dad. He hoped his parents would stay together for a long time.

They were talking loudly in the kitchen last night after Dad came home from his evening patrol. It was late, and their voices woke him up. He was afraid that they might be arguing about whether he was old enough to go deer hunting. But after a while, he could tell that they were not talking about him or about hunting, although he'd heard his name once. They didn't seem to be fighting. Maybe they would stay together.

Another sharp, sudden *crunch* broke his reverie. Hooves? No. The sound was too loud. A voice? Dad said he might use a grunt call if he needed to. "If you think you hear me," he'd said, "be patient. Sound carries a long way in the woods. I might be close by, or I might not. Don't lift the bow until you see horns. Be sure."

Crunch.

Not hooves. But what? Two bucks fighting! Or was his father carrying a set of rattling horns? Luke couldn't remember. No, it was voices. Dad said he might use his voice to move the deer if they stopped for too long. Luke cocked his head and strained to hear. Adrenaline coursed through his slim, pre-adolescent body. Without thinking, and almost as if he were watching someone else, he felt himself stand and lift the bow and then pull the bowstring back to full draw. His dad had said to be still and remain patient. "Don't lift the bow until you see horns," he'd said. But it felt right to be ready.

Soon though, Luke's thin, unmuscled arms began to quiver and the bow shake. He realized then that he could not hold the bow at full draw for very long and that he would have to put it down. As he was thinking that, brush moved further down the gully, and something passed behind a tree. Horns? His dad had warned him that branches could look like horns. Luke's arms began to tremble and the bow to vibrate like a tuning fork. He could not hold it steady. Easing his grip was the second rookie mistake. The released tension transferred immediately from the hand holding the bow to the fingers of the opposite hand that held the bowstring. Just like that, he heard and felt the *whoosh!* of an arrow launched through the air at lethal speed. He could not have held it back.

Then came a shout, or more accurately, a curse word. Luke's heart surged. He felt frightened and sick. Dropping the bow, he unbuckled the tree harness, scraping his hands and face against the rough tree bark as he scrambled out of the tree and ran toward the sound. Up ahead, a man lay on his side, a blood-covered hand pressed to his lower back and the other hand clamped to his front. Luke was afraid to move closer. The sound of dry wood snapping nearby made him turn his head. Someone dressed in green and brown camo was running downhill fast. The runner's head was covered by a tan billed cap, with a flap in the back like the Japanese soldiers wore in old WWII movies. The man must have seen what had happened and was going for help. Or maybe to get the police. Luke tried to shout, but no sound came from his mouth. He tried to run after the fleeing figure, but he slipped on a patch of dead leaves, and his face plowed the soft earth. He thought he heard another voice. But he couldn't be sure. He couldn't see his dad or hear him. He tried to shout, but still no sound came. Scrambling to his feet, he ran toward the voice, or voices. He was scared. He had accidentally shot someone, and they needed help. But he was all turned around, and he didn't know where he was. He didn't know where his dad was.

* * *

Joe Morgan struggled to remove his blood-soaked shirt and roll it into something he could use as a compression bandage. He hadn't seen or heard anything before the sudden, searing pain of a razor-edged broadhead, arrow shaft, and stiff, plastic fletching passing through his body. As soon as he'd managed to settle his heartbeat, recover his breath, and plug the entry and exit wounds with torn strips of shirt, he crawled toward the tree stand where he had left his son. Maybe some myopic hunter hadn't been able to tell the difference between a four-legged herbivore and a grown man dressed in camouflage. Or maybe some maniac had decided to reprise *The Most Dangerous Game*. Either way, Joe knew that he had to find his son, get back to the truck, and get to a hospital, fast.

Fear and anger fueled his stumble toward the tree stand where he had left his son, and he passed out twice before the stand became visible through the mixed pine and hardwood. When he recovered consciousness, he saw that the boy was not where he had left him. Staggering across the loam below the tree stand, he looked for blood but found only his own. Then he saw a line of bent and trampled burdock that seemed to form a zigzag trail leading downhill. *The kid probably heard me and climbed down from the tree stand. What would he have done when he didn't find me? Head toward the truck? Panic? Get lost?* Joe hoped his son hadn't panicked. There wasn't time.

Staggering from tree to tree, around and over blowdowns and ditches, he fell twice, disgorging meatball-sized clots of coagulated blood from the entry and exit wounds. He briefly lost consciousness after the second fall. Then coming to, he saw a glint of sunlight behind a copse of trees. Staggering to his feet, he stumbled toward the light and found Luke sitting on the ground beside the truck, arms wrapped around his legs, shaking.

The boy stood as his father stumbled toward him, though he didn't step forward or speak. "Hey, buddy," Joe gasped. "I need your help." He reached into the front pocket of his blood-covered pants and handed the truck keys to his son. "Open the door and put these in the ignition. I'll climb up after you if I can."

The boy remained immobile.

"Luke, unlock the truck and get inside."

Luke started to tremble and then to cry.

"LUKE! MOVE!!!"

* * *

Bonnie Morgan sat quietly in an over-stuffed chair in the main room of the five thousand square foot, split-log cabin that her family called home. Surrounded by ten acres of sloping field and mixed hardwood, the massive home enjoyed a panoramic view of Coldwater Lake at this time of year. Wrapping her hands around a warm ceramic cup that had been made by one of her children in summer art class, she took a sip of the hot liquid and eased into a rare moment of solitude. She needed it. The girls were at school, and Luke was off in the woods with his dad. She was not happy that her husband had taken their son out of school for the opening day of archery deer season. They had had words about it. Though, as usual, her husband had gotten his way. Few people could say no to Joe Morgan and make it stick. Those, like Bonnie, who occasionally managed the feat, eventually discovered that saying no had no lasting effect. Joe Morgan was a force of nature who easily overpowered with his physical presence and chilling demeanor. Bonnie had learned to pick her battles. Pulling Luke out of school once a year for the opening day of archery deer season wasn't the right battle, and it was not worth the price she would have to pay for antagonizing the bear.

Luke had been doing well at school since she brought him and his sisters back to Coldwater. He seemed happy, though he rarely spoke except in response to a direct question. The girls seemed reasonably content. Sisters on the cusp of adolescence, they kept busy with soccer, sleepovers and gossip about boys. Meghan, the oldest, suffered a violent crush on a new young man at least every other week. Kate, who was eighteen months younger, kept her own counsel. Bonnie felt that bringing her children back to Coldwater had been the right thing to do—for them. For her, it remained a stressful mix of fading hope, strategic retreat, and reluctant acceptance.

Seeing a marriage counselor with Joe had been one of her conditions for returning with the kids. With the help of a professional, she had been able to talk freely about the dangers of her husband's job and the corrosive effect that constant worry had on their relationship and family. Joe had been dutiful in attending the weekly sessions. But he had little to say other than to point out that he'd been a cop before they were married and before they decided to have children. His view was that he had never hidden or minimized the demands of his job and that his wife knew what she was getting into when she married him. As for "the other stuff," he'd promised that there would be no more of that. So, as far as he was concerned, there was nothing more to talk about.

But the question of whether to stay and under what conditions wasn't closed for Bonnie. Her husband may have been right that she knew what she was getting into when she married him. But the kids didn't choose to be born into a family where their father goes to work every day at a job he might not come home from. Joe had had enough close brushes with death in recent years to make it obvious that sooner or later, he almost certainly would not come home. Or at least not in one piece.

Luke was almost five before he started to speak. The doctors had not been able to identify a cause for the developmental delay. But a mother's instinct told Bonnie that fear—perhaps picked up from her and the girls—played an important role, an unspoken dread that when their father left the house in the morning with a heavy, black 9mm Glock strapped to his side, there was a real possibility that he might not come home at the end of the day.

Bonnie rolled the ceramic cup between her hands. It had grown cold during her musings, and she felt chill even though it was a mild and windless fall day. Joe may have been right that no one put a gun to her head when she decided to marry him and later have children with him. But whatever she had agreed to years ago had been in ignorance. The responsible thing now was to take a clear-eyed look at the life they were leading and do what was best for everyone, most importantly for the children. "Best" could not be to do nothing. As her father used to say, 'Hope is not a strategy.'

When the phone rang, she assumed it was one of the girls calling to be picked up from soccer practice. She grabbed a handful of snacks from the kitchen and the car keys from the wooden peg beside the wall phone and then picked up the receiver.

"Mrs. Morgan?" The speaker's tone and the familiar hospital clatter in the background caused Bonnie to reach for the edge of the laminated countertop. "This is Doctor Tran at the Coldwater Emergency Room."

"Yes?" Her throat felt suddenly constricted, and her voice cracked.

"Your husband was admitted to the hospital a few minutes ago. He's in surgery now."

She reached for one of the counter stools and sat down heavily. "My son was with him." she managed to breathe. "Is he hurt, too?"

The was a pause at the other end of the line and some muffled voices. Then another voice spoke into the phone. "Mrs. Morgan, this is Nurse Mulvey. A boy came in with your husband, but we haven't been able to identify him or get him to say anything. He's not hurt."

Bonnie struggled to find a coherent voice.

"Mrs. Morgan?"

"Yes," she whispered. "What is the boy wearing?"

There was another long pause, and then, "Camouflage pants and a beige Carhartt jacket. Is that what your son was wearing?"

"Yes." Her voice regained a measure of strength. "You said he's not hurt?"

"There's no apparent physical injury. But he may be in shock. He's not responding to questions. Can I tell him that his mother is on the way?"

"Yes. Please. I'm getting into the car now."

* * *

Later, Bonnie didn't remember calling her mother-in-law to ask her to stay with the girls, or driving to the hospital, or trying without success to get Luke to talk about what had happened. When she arrived at the Coldwater Hospital, she saw a uniformed state trooper standing in the hallway near the nurses' station talking with one of the emergency room doctors. A second state trooper sat next to Luke in the waiting room. Bonnie went to her son and knelt on the cold floor in front of his chair. "Are you all right?" she asked. She hugged her son softly and then pulled back to search his face.

The boy did not answer or look up.

"Are you hurt?" She placed a hand on his camouflage pants. They were smeared with damp blood. He shook his head. "Do you know what happened to Dad?"

The boy lifted his legs so that his heels rested on the edge of the hard plastic chair. Then he wrapped his arms around his shins and began to moan softly.

The trooper sitting in the chair next to Luke closed his cloth-covered notebook and turned toward Bonnie. "Are you the boy's mother?"

"Yes."

"I need to ask him some questions."

"Now?" She glared at him.

The trooper, who had been in the hallway speaking with one of the doctors, broke off his conversation and entered the waiting room. His hands remained at his side. "I'm so sorry, Mrs. Morgan."

She stood. "Oh. Paulie, I'm glad it's you. Where have they taken Joe? What's happened to him?"

"Sheriff Morgan is in surgery. It appears that he's suffered a wound from a hunting arrow."

Bonnie lifted a hand to her mouth. "Did he fall? He was out bowhunting with Luke."

The trooper looked down at the boy. "We don't know what happened yet. I'm hoping Luke here can tell us."

Bonnie dropped to her knees again and placed her hands on her son's shoulders. "Luke, honey, do you know what happened to your father? Did he fall out of a tree?" Luke squeezed his legs and buried his face in the V between his knees. He did not look up. Bonnie turned her face to the trooper. "He still gets like this sometimes."

"I'm sorry," said the trooper. "But we'll need to speak with him as soon as possible."

* * *

Bonnie left Luke with the two state troopers and went to look for the doctor who the trooper, Paulie Grogan, had been speaking to outside the waiting room. When she found him, she got a bunch of medical-speak about entry and exit wounds and organs pierced and not pierced, but not much about Joe's outlook for recovery. He would remain sedated and unconscious for several hours.

While she tried to figure out what to do next, she thought about calling Joe's brother. Tom and Joe Morgan were estranged, Joe having punched out his brother's front teeth several months ago in a temporary resolution to a long-simmering family dispute. Tom had gone to Europe soon after that and had not returned. Bonnie had tried to contact him several times. In part, to learn what had happened between him and Joe, to see if it could be fixed, and to find out if he was okay. But also, because in times of crisis, her brother-in-law was the only rational, non-belligerent member of the Morgan family, and she feared losing that anchor of stability. Tom Morgan was also the only person who could get through to Luke when things got bad. But since leaving for Europe, he had not answered or returned any of her calls. And, of course, neither Joe nor his mother would even mention Tom's name.

But Joe's getting shot was something her brother-in-law needed to know, family squabble or no. She looked at her watch. It would be 9:30 pm in London where he was living now—too early for him to have gone to bed. She dialed his number, heard it ring, and then listened to an anonymous English-accented voice invite her to leave a message.

Chapter Two

Several floors below Tom Morgan's office and across the cobbled street, barristers in white wigs and black gowns crisscrossed the quadrangle of Middle Temple, looking like extras in a 1930s black-and-white historical drama. Men had been making deals on this patch of Central London for over eight hundred years, and Tom felt happy to be one of them, back in the game that had made him wealthy before his fortieth birthday.

Pacing in front of a conference room window, he went over what he hoped to accomplish on the upcoming phone call. He had come to London to create a futures market for European films. Though the concept was as old as the practice of selling next year's crop to pay for this year's seed, nothing like it had been done before, either in the United States or in Europe. If the exchange developed as he'd envisioned, players would be able to trade financial instruments tied to the box office performance of individual films, as well as various combinations of actors, directors, and studios. The financial resources that market would provide could help Europe's film industry compete better with Hollywood. But assembling the necessary pieces was proving time-consuming and contentious.

The list of unanticipated obstacles seemed to grow daily. The most recent was a sudden lack of support from the project's corporate sponsor and Tom's law firm. Tom had put nearly all his liquid assets into the project as seed money. So, any hint that the project's backers were having second thoughts was more than troubling. He had thought long and hard about taking such a large risk. And he had sought the advice of the smartest and most successful businessmen he knew before committing his personal funds. Each had given the same warning. The brass ring only comes around once. If you don't grab it, you may regret it forever. But if you've already made a pile, and going after a bigger one requires that you risk everything you've already made, then you'd better be certain that the bet will pay off. Because it's difficult enough to make the first fortune. Few get a chance to make a second.

It had not been an easy decision. But in the end, he decided to do it. But as time passed and problems mounted, it was hard to avoid second-guessing. The upside remained compelling. But multiplying sources of possible failure all lay with people and organizations outside his control. Each had his or its own agenda, and none shared Tom's personal financial risk. By nature cool and unflappable—a trait, that occasionally unsettled bosses, competitors, and significant others alike— he was keenly aware that this project would dramatically change his life. But in which direction?

The corporate sponsor, a major New York bond dealer, had a desperate need to offload excess computer capacity that it had purchased at the peak of the market. But the company's chairman was as risk-averse as his bond-buying customers when it came to the day-to-day decision-making on issues related to the project launch. Primarily motivated by the need to cover up his ill-timed capital investment, the details and complexities of a project that might save his job and reputation seemed only to render him more anxious and indecisive.

The managing partner of Tom's law firm was presenting a different problem. Tanner Hartwell was not uncomfortable with risk, but he had a patrician's distaste for financial speculation. In addition to his personal investment, Tom's plan for a European film exchange called for his law firm to take an equity position in the exchange in lieu of billing for services, as was traditional as well as prudent. It was an arrangement that the firm's managing partner had several times disparaged as gambling rather than practicing law, and his support for the project had diminished with each unanticipated difficulty.

What Tom was about to propose was unlikely to be embraced, either by his firm or the project sponsor, and suggesting it might prove to be the slippery slope to professional *seppuku*. But it had to be done. Launching a new kind of financial exchange was a complex undertaking that required time and financial breathing room to get off the ground. Proceeding too fast or without sufficient and coordinated resources would almost certainly lead to disaster.

"The market looks like it's going to close down a thousand points," said Hartwell as soon as he picked up the phone. "Give me some good news."

Tom had anticipated the question and had prepared a suitable, if misleading, answer.

"I'm meeting with each of the major European film distributors this week. Paris tonight, Berlin tomorrow, back on Wednesday." The scratch of a pen on paper an ocean away was as clear as if Hartwell had been sitting in the next room. The major mobile phone services were improving every year, but halfway through the first decade of the new century, the quality was not yet up to that of landlines. Until then, Tom preferred to make his more important calls from his office.

"Will the exchange be operational by the end of the year?" asked Hartwell.

You know the answer as well as I do, thought Tom. He let the silence linger before throwing his boss a bone. "If we can bypass regulatory approval."

"How do you propose to do that?"

"By purchasing an existing exchange whose charter allows it to expand into other lines of businesses."

The scratching stopped. "You want to buy the London Stock Exchange?"

The tone was sarcastic, but Tom treated the question as if it were serious if only to keep Hartwell focused on facts rather than fears. "Too big. We need something small that won't make headlines when we take it over. Done quietly, it should cut two years and three hundred million euros off the cost."

"We?"

Quit yanking my chain.

"The client, Tanner. I've already broken my piggy bank to get this thing started. The film exchange is their rescue plan, not mine. If it isn't launched on solid financial footing, it's their balance sheet that will hit the fan first."

Tom didn't like to stress the rescue point. He was excited about the project on its own merits because it was large, lucrative, challenging, and needed. He cared less about pulling a client's financial cookies out of the fire, even if that was Tanner's primary, if not sole, objective. Tom tried to avoid highlighting their differences whenever possible. But as time went on, it was becoming more difficult.

"And how much will this 'too small to notice' thing cost?" Hartwell prompted.

I don't know. We haven't found it yet.

Tom took a moment to find a diplomatic response. "I'll get you a figure as soon as we've identified a target. But whatever it costs, it will be a fraction of what we'll have to spend if we're forced to go the regulatory route in multiple European jurisdictions."

This time, it was Hartwell who let the silence linger. "I'll have to get back to you, Tom."

* * *

The phone call from Tom's sister-in-law came shortly after Tom got on the line with Hartwell. A second call followed minutes later, and the third came soon after that. Tom let all three calls go to voice mail. His sister-in-law had tried to reach him several times since he left Coldwater, and he had yet to answer or return any of her calls. He did not wish to be rude. But there was nothing new to say. He saw no point pretending to maintain a *status quo ante* with the wife of the brother who had knocked out Tom's front teeth for having the temerity to ask hard questions about their father's death.

Still, three phone calls in the space of an hour without leaving a message might mean something serious. Maybe something with one of the kids. Tom wished his sister-in-law had left a voicemail. From the back seat of a black cab on his way to Gatwick Airport, Tom found himself punching the return call button on his mobile. *Guilt: the gift that keeps on giving.* "It's Tom," he said when the line opened. "You've been trying to reach me?"

The voice on the other side of the ocean was weak and almost without intonation. "Tom?"

"Yes, Bonnie. I'm returning your call."

"Tom. Your brother's been shot."

Chapter Three

Tom paid off the cab at the airport Departures entrance and dropped his overnight bag on a gray concrete bench near the curb. In an unsteady voice, his sister-in-law shared the few details she had. "He's in surgery. Someone shot him through the back with an arrow."

"A what?"

"He was out in the woods with Luke. The doctors say that he's lost a lot of blood."

Tom's voice trembled. "Was Luke hurt?"

"No. But he's not talking again."

Tom's nephew had been almost five years old before he started to speak. Batteries of medical tests had failed to pinpoint the cause of the developmental delay. Now, nearly eleven, he occasionally lapsed into unexplained periods of silence.

"The surgeon said that the arrow missed the vital organs," Bonne continued. "He said that if Joe can avoid infection, he has a good chance of recovery." She paused and then repeated, "But he's lost a lot of blood."

Tom looked up at the departure board and saw that his plane would begin boarding in a few minutes. "My brother's a tough man, Bonnie. If the doctors say he's got a good chance to recover, he'll be out faster than they think."

"I don't know, Tom."

"What do they say about Luke's not talking?"

"I haven't... Not with Joe..." His sister-in-law left the sentence unfinished. "How soon can you get here?"

It was the question that Tom had hoped to avoid as his answer was unlikely to be understood or accepted. *Don't let the door hit you in the butt,* was more or less the way his brother and mother had expressed their goodbyes when they effectively banished Tom from Coldwater several months ago. The long-simmering tension between the brother who stayed home and followed in their father's footsteps and the one who left for the big city and broader horizons had finally boiled over into an actual fistfight. It wasn't their first all-out brawl. But it was their first as grown men. And the new set of front teeth that greeted Tom in the bathroom mirror each morning was a daily reminder of who had prevailed.

For reasons that Tom still didn't quite understand, or perhaps didn't care to, their mother had appeared to welcome the physical resolution to the long-simmering family tension and had shown no hesitation in picking sides. That, as much as anything else, had helped Tom make up his mind about what future role, if any, his *family* would play in his life. After much thought and more guilt, he had decided that while he might return to Coldwater for the obligatory wedding or funeral, he was otherwise done with the violent, alcoholic, misogynistic, superstition-masquerading-as-religion, corrupt to the core Morgan clan. Done, done, and completely done.

"Joe doesn't want me there, Bonnie," he finally answered. "Neither does our mother. I know you must need help. But mine wouldn't be welcome. If I came, it would only add to your troubles."

"Tom! Your brother's been shot. How can you not come home?"

"It's not my home anymore, Bonnie."

* * *

How long had Coldwater not been his home? Since he went away to college? Or before, when he started to date Susan Pearce and had his first exposure to a world beyond the horizon and values of the punch the clock and anything else that got in your way Morgan clan? He certainly knew it by the time MadDog was murdered, and Tom and his brother found stacks of one-hundred-dollar bills stuffed into the lining of the suitcoat their father was to be buried in. For Tom, that hidden stash had confirmed what he had long suspected: MadDog Morgan, the larger-than-life father of Tom's terrorized childhood, was just another cop on the take.

But it was longer than that before Tom accepted that Coldwater was no longer home and could never be again. A few years ago, when his brother got Tom involved in the investigation of a pair of local murders, the combination of Tom's legal and financial skills and Joe's investigation expertise proved effective in solving the cases. But Joe's methods: whatever it took to get what he wanted, including violence, disturbed Tom greatly. It appeared that Joe was on the fast track to becoming just like their father. And no good would come of that.

For the moment, however, Tom had escaped. Living in London, he felt content to be well-compensated for doing what he enjoyed and excelled at. But London was not home, and he sometimes found himself reflecting on his friend Father Gauss's admonition that making money was a useful skill, but it was not a life. He had the one. But the other, so far, had proven elusive. It had been true for a long time now.

For the last portion of the hour and twenty-minute flight to Paris, Tom tried to distract himself from the issues raised by Bonnie's troubling phone call by returning his attention to the ostensible reason for his being and staying in Europe. The notes he had collected on Yvette Huppe filled a fat accordion file and a large manila envelope. The file contained copies of articles and interviews in Paris Match and other popular magazines. The envelope held a confidential report from the Paris office of Kroll Associates, the well-known commercial investigation service. According to the Kroll report, the woman Tom was to meet for dinner was the *Directrice Général* of France's second oldest film distributor, Clement Frères, granddaughter of its founder, and a graduate of the prestigious *Institut Européen d'Administration des Affaires.* Madame Huppe was known in the industry as a skillful guardian of her family's legacy, determined to keep management control of the business in family hands. Of necessity, she spent much of her time pursuing commercial and financial alliances needed to maintain that control, and it was rumored that she was wearying of the task. Tom's goal for the evening was to persuade *Madame la Directrice* that a European film futures exchange might help to ease her burden.

The chauffeur sent to meet Tom's plane brought him to a trendy restaurant on *Rue Quincampois,* known for serving its food in near darkness to provide its patrons with a Michelin-quality gustatory experience without visual distraction. The lack of illumination in *Dans le Noir* reminded Tom that Ben Franklin, in Paris to raise funds for the American Revolution, had invented the bifocal there after discovering his self-taught Yankee French required him to read lips in order to get through a typical candle-lit French dinner party. At least Tom would be alone with Madame Huppe, and from the Kroll photos, it did not appear that lip reading would be a hardship.

The *chef serveur* led Tom through an unlit maze of close tables to one in the farthest corner. The lone occupant remained seated and extended her hand. Tom leaned over to kiss it. *"Enchanté."*

"Quebecois?"

"New York."

"Ah. Then we will speak English."

Linguistic one-upmanship established, Madame Huppe omitted the polite, 'How was your flight,' small talk, and instead launched into a succinct overview of her family business and her reason for taking the meeting. While she spoke, Tom tried to shake intrusive thoughts about what was going on an ocean away. *Joe had been shot. Or had he? Could Mr. Outdoorsman have fallen on his own arrow? Or had some cuckold husband taken advantage of a dark woods encounter to loose a payback arrow?*

Tom told himself that it didn't matter. It had nothing to do with him now. Though allowing Joe's impalement to intrude on an important business meeting made the assertion suspect. Returning his attention to his dinner companion, he eased into his prepared pitch at the appropriate opening. The French businesswoman listened without comment. Then, when he had finished, she raised the same issue that he had earlier discussed with Tanner Hartwell.

"There is much regulation in France, Monsieur Morgan, especially in the arts."

"And frustration with the hurdles it takes to produce quality French film."

Tom had anticipated the objection, though the solution he'd pitched to the managing partner of his law firm was not one he could share with this French film distributor. He answered instead with a summary of the several financial benefits that would accrue to any participating film distributor.

"And regulation?"

"A challenge. But not insurmountable."

Madame Huppe made a disbelieving face. "And what prevents this film exchange from trying to take over the distribution business? By setting expensive standards, for example."

It was a valid concern, and admitting it was the only honest answer. But he did so obliquely.

"No one will pay for an inferior product," he said. "But if you're worried about the film exchange using quality control as a proxy for management control, then license your data to the studios and the public, not just to the exchange. If you spread the money out, no single licensee will have the power to dictate what you provide, when, or for how much."

Madame Huppe waved a hand in the air over the barely visible tablecloth. "Another distributor will eventually meet such demands, no?"

"Then the risk to Clement Frères will be foregone revenue, not loss of management control. That decision would remain in your hands, always."

Madame Huppe leaned back in her seat. Tom watched her face. She was of the May '68 generation whose student rioters had caused Charles de Gaulle to secretly flee to West Germany when his country and government appeared on the verge of collapse. They were a breed unto themselves and not to be underestimated. "You are not the salesman, Monsieur Morgan. But I can see you have thought of these things. *C'est bon.*"

The switch to French appeared to signal that the business was over for the moment. The quick transition made Tom suspect that Madame Huppe had made up her mind before taking the meeting and that Clement Frères might be strapped for cash or have other pressing problems. According to Kroll, the larger French distributors were adequately supplied with Hollywood films for the coming year. But the commercial investigation service had not been able to uncover what the distributors had given to secure that pipeline.

Madame Huppe signaled to the waiter and ordered a vodka martini.

"Perrier," said Tom.

"You do not drink?"

"Not regularly."

The look she gave Tom was familiar. The days of the three-martini lunch were long over in the United States. But a certain amount of alcohol consumption remained an important part of business socializing in Europe. Tom was not a teetotaler. But he usually refrained from alcohol while doing business.

"And the other pleasures of life?" Madame Huppe pursued. "Do you deny yourself those, as well?"

"I'm told that moderation has its benefits." As he said this, a pair of Parisian hotties passed close by their table, and when one brushed Tom's shoulder with her *derrière,* he did not look up.

Madame Huppe's eyes seemed to reassess her dinner companion. Inclining her head toward the narrow space vacated by passing women, she asked or commented, he wasn't sure, "You are moderate in such things, as well?"

He smiled and bowed his head. "For the moment, I just work."

"But that is unhealthy, Monsieur Morgan!"

Tom folded his hands and leaned away from the table. "If we're going to talk about my lack of social life, perhaps you should call me Tom."

Madame Huppe laughed. "*Bien.* Yvette. But why no social life, Tom? You are handsome, wealthy and your gentlemanly assessment shows that you do not limit your appreciation to *les ingénue* only."

"Busted."

"*Comment?* My bust?"

Tom laughed. "Sorry. 'Busted' is American slang for an unintended disclosure."

"Ah!" Madame Huppe paused, no doubt committing this new American idiom to her English lexicon. "And my question?"

"Lack of time, I suppose."

"That is an excuse, not an answer."

Tom looked briefly away from the table and took a moment to respond.

The risks of sharing personal confidences with a business acquaintance of less than an hour were obvious. But the opportunity to explore an interesting topic with a presumably knowledgeable member of the opposite gender was tempting. Such opportunities did not present themselves often in Tom's busy life, and he was inclined to take advantage. "All right," he said. "But stop me if this gets too abstract."

"*Bien.*"

"Would you agree that adult relationships begin with attraction and chemistry?"

Madame Huppe compressed her lips causing a pair of oval-shaped dimples to appear on her cheeks. "Attraction, yes. Chemistry, of course. But there is much more."

"Agreed. Most importantly, values. But those can take time to uncover."

Yvette waited.

"This may sound unromantic. But I suspect that values are what determine the success or failure of a relationship in the long run—assuming attraction and chemistry remain."

"*Sérieusement?*"

"I think so."

Yvette smiled. "You must persuade me."

"Alright. Say you've begun a new relationship. You and your new partner have attraction and chemistry, and from conversation it appears that you share the common values of family, ambition, and adventure."

"*Bon.*"

"But then one of you is presented with an ideal career opportunity. Say, an obscenely well-paid executive position in Dubai."

"Yes?"

"Then you discover that while you share the same values, you hold them in a different order. The partner who received the attractive career offer values ambition, adventure, and family in that order, and he or she would happily leave extended family and friends to take the perfect job. The other partner, though he or she shares those same values, puts family first and ambition second. He or she would never consider leaving their extended family and cherished business in Paris."

"I see."

"Sadly, the crises that reveal divergent values don't necessarily come early in a relationship. One can be happy for a long time in a stew of attraction and chemistry until a conflict arises to reveal some fundamental incompatibility."

"Un philosophe!"

Tom lifted his hands.

"And is family one of your values, Tom?"

"No."

Huppe's head drew back as if she'd been slapped.

And this is why sharing personal confidences with a new business acquaintance is risky. His dinner companion folded her hands on the tablecloth and waited for Tom to extricate his foot from his mouth.

"I'm sorry, Yvette. But we don't choose our families. Unlike yours, mine is not a source of pride. I distance myself from them. It's not a happy choice, but it's a necessary one."

Madame Huppe remained silent and then switched abruptly back to English and business. "When will you meet with the German and UK distributors?"

You blew it, buddy.

"I meet with Karlheinz Klopp in Baden-Baden tomorrow," he answered, following her retreat to safer ground. "Afterward with Cedric Fulton in London."

"Then, may I make a suggestion?"

"Please."

"You can travel from city to city making these little dinners. But I think you must do *le weekend* if you wish to make progress."

"Le weekend?"

"At a nice country house. To bring the necessary players together for a few days—for talk, dinner, a little flirting, perhaps."

"Do you have such a place?"

"One can be arranged. But we are agreed that Clement Frères would supply data to the exchange customers, as you suggest, not to the film exchange exclusively?"

Tom nodded absently. *"D'accord."* The mention of a country house weekend had momentarily snapped his head back to his phone call with Bonnie. *Had she said shot, or wounded? Joe must have fallen. You can't shoot yourself in the back with an arrow.*

Seeing Tom's distraction and noting his switch back to French, Madame Huppe politely inquired where his head had gone. Was there a problem with the business agreement?

"I'm sorry," Tom apologized. "The business is fine. But I'm a bit distracted. Shortly before I arrived here, I received a phone call from my sister-in-law in the United States. My brother has been in a hunting accident."

"Oh! I am sorry. Is he hurt?"

"He's in the hospital."

"Then you must go to him! We need not sit here discussing business any longer. That is settled, I think."

"It is, as far as I'm concerned. But my brother would undoubtedly prefer that I stay here."

She looked at him closely. "You are estranged?"

"Busted again."

"Enough of my bust! You must return to your family in such times!"

Tom sought his dinner companion's eyes through the dim light. "My brother is a corrupt policeman with a violent temper and a taste for women other than the one he's married to. My hopping on an airplane to tell him he should be more careful in the woods is not a good use of my time. Your idea of *le weekend* is. Why don't we order dessert and discuss who we need to invite?"

Chapter Four

Bonnie stepped into a hospital service elevator, padded and large enough to hold several gurneys at the same time. At the third floor, she followed an antiseptic-smelling hallway decorated with schoolchildren's art to the Intensive Care Unit where Joe was recuperating. On the way, she muttered a wish that her mother-in-law would not be there. ICU patients were allowed only one visitor at a time, and Mary Morgan had hardly left her son's side since he'd been wheeled into the hospital on a blood-soaked gurney eighteen hours before.

Bonnie had always struggled to understand her mother-in-law's relationship with her two sons. Mary Morgan made no effort to disguise the fact that Joe was her favorite. Though why that should be was not obvious. Of course, he was handsome, virile and charming—qualities that Bonnie had once found irresistible and that other women apparently still did. But mothers usually take a wider view and weigh other criteria. Yet with Mary's undisguised blessing, Joe had brutally driven his older brother away from Coldwater and circled the wagons around *his* town and *his* family. Bonnie did not know what had happened between the brothers, or why. There had been a fight. A real one. With Tom needing stitches and a new set of front teeth when it was over. But neither Mary nor Joe would talk about it. All Bonnie knew for certain was that her brother-in-law had moved to London, and that, from the little he had said on their brief, unsatisfying phone call, he intended to stay there.

With Mary and Joe maintaining a united silence, Bonnie saw little point in pursuing unpopular questions. More important to her was that she and

Joe begin to make progress in their couples therapy. So far, there'd been none. Joe had been dutiful in attending the sessions. But it was clear that he went there looking for relief, not change. He was nowhere close to facing the truth that the job of Coldwater Sheriff would sooner or later leave him dead and his family destitute. Or that his self-centered philandering was destroying their marriage. It was only a question of which avoidable tragedy imploded the family first.

Bonnie tried to push these troubling thoughts aside as entered Joe's hospital room. There, perched on the edge of a green plastic chair by the side of Joe's bed, a hunched Mary Morgan sat gripping her son's hand in both of hers, pleading in a hushed whisper that carried as well as if she had been shouting. "You've got to tell me where it is, Joe."

"Where what is?" asked Bonnie, approaching the bed.

Mary looked up, startled. "What are you doing here?"

"Hoping to spend time with my husband."

Mary stood. "He's not well, you know."

Bonnie suppressed a rejoinder along the lines of "Duh!" while she watched her mother-in-law pitch a long, worried look in her son's direction, gather her bags, and then exit the room without greeting or goodbye.

Bonnie had long ago accepted her mother-in-law's curiously limited range of emotion and empathy, as well as her complete lack of social graces. She wanted what she wanted, and she usually got it. While Bonnie and the kids had been staying with Bonnie's parents across the lake in Canada, what Mary wanted was her grandchildren back in Coldwater. Now that she'd gotten that, she was onto the next thing—her son's recovery. Bonnie didn't begrudge her mother-in-law's priorities, only her myopia in how she pursued them. In Bonnie's experience, getting what you want and keeping it often requires opposite efforts. Aggressive pursuit followed by collaborative fence mending, for example. Mary and her youngest son were unequaled in the former. But neither were any good at the latter.

She sometimes wondered if mother and son's extreme behavior might have been a consequence of their striking physical presence. A muscular six foot four, two hundred and forty-five pounds, Joe was a modern-day Paul

Bunyan who looked every bit as intimidating as he, in fact, was. Men and women couldn't help but respond accordingly. Mary was one of those natural beauties whose striking good looks had become even more compelling with age. The lioness's head of thick dark hair had long since turned white, but the porcelain skin remained firm and flawless. Mary had never used or needed makeup. And neither age nor drink had made a visible dent in her handsome presence. At times, Bonnie felt jealous. She wondered if mother and son might have been easier to get along with had they not been so physically blessed.

Taking her mother-in-law's vacated spot, Bonnie reached a tentative hand toward her husband's. His eyes remained shut, but the pressure from his fingers told her he was awake. "I'm here," she said. The fingers squeezed. Maybe she should feel guilty, but in that moment she felt something like relief. Could there be any argument now about how dangerous Joe's job was? Three life-threatening assaults and hospitalizations in four years—one from poisoning, another from a gun ambush, and this latest from an apparent arrow through the back. Bonnie had no desire to become a policeman's widow—the hero's wife, attractive but no longer young, broke, and with three kids. Surely, Joe would see now that she could not go on like this and that he should not ask her to.

Bonnie had once thought that she could have everything she wanted with Joe Morgan, a handsome rogue who appeared to love his family and who was clearly capable of protecting them. But fifteen years into their marriage, the only part that had proven true was his qualified love of family—conditioned on their forbearance with his chosen lifestyle which included both opportunistic dalliances and the real possibility that sooner or later he might be killed on the job and no longer be around to protect and provide for them. For Bonnie, both the casual philandering and the careless flirtation with death were no longer acceptable. But what were her options? What was realistically available beyond her current role as a long-suffering wife and isolated mother? How could she provide her children with a better life than they now had, make sure that they were safe, and break the chain of passive Morgan mothers who put up with whatever their husbands felt entitled to dish out? How could she accomplish that? By leaving? For where? To do what?

All she knew for certain was that she had to do something. Waiting for Joe to get himself killed and then suffering the kind of abrupt, uncontrolled, and unpleasant change that would surely fall on her and her children then, was irresponsible and dangerous. It was long since time to act, though the list of practical obstacles was intimidating. Whatever she did now, to act or acquiesce, had to put their children first. Though her choices seemed limited to accepting her role as wife and mother to a corrupt, philandering rogue, winning the lotto, waiting for a white knight to appear, or managing alone as a single mom by finding some way to survive and prosper with her children in Coldwater. Except for possibly winning the lotto, none of those options inspired.

Realistically, she had no desire to be a single mom, especially in Coldwater—a picturesque but far from prosperous little town a few cold nautical miles from the Canadian border. Leaving was a constant temptation. But she had tried that once, and her parents had made it clear that living with them in Canada was not a permanent solution. Their house was small, they were not wealthy, and the kids, especially Luke, hated it there. Even if she could stay in Coldwater, breaking up a family when the kids were young was something she was reluctant to do. Live in public housing? Take some low-paying job just to put food on the table? The girls growing up surrounded by...what?

Without a meaningful job or someone suitable to fill the role of husband, father, and provider, the immediate future for her and her children looked sad and depressing. But sitting beside Joe's bed, holding a calloused hand that had done God knows what to whom and how often, Bonnie could not quite bring herself to pull the plug. Not yet. Not without something better.

As she sat there fretting about her family's future, Dr. Tran entered the room and told her that it might be another few hours before Joe regained consciousness. "Your husband is out of immediate danger," he said. "I've given him something to keep him from moving so that the internal stitching has time to take hold. I've also put him on intravenous antibiotics. If he remains reasonably still and manages to avoid infection, he should experience a full recovery. Your husband a remarkable physical specimen, Mrs. Morgan. And incredibly lucky."

Only the good die young.

As long as Joe would remain unconscious for a few hours, Bonnie decided to walk to his office in the basement of Town Hall to retrieve his laptop and whatever else might be on his desk. From previous hospitalizations, she knew that he would want all of it as soon as he woke and that he would ask her to get it. It was something to do and a way to be useful until she knew more and could do more, and until she made up her mind about what to do next.

Outside the hospital, fallen leaves blew in tight swirls across the sidewalk and the chill air smelled of autumn. On the short walk to Town Hall, she tried her brother-in-law's phone one more time, swearing under her breath when her call went to voice mail. That Joe's brother didn't answer her calls was no longer a surprise. What was, was how angry that made her feel. Tom Morgan, international lawyer, and deal maker—or whatever it was he did, she was never sure—had the luxury of running away. Bonnie Morgan, homemaker and mother of three, didn't.

She usually avoided visiting her Joe's office, a musty, ill-lit warren in the basement of a clapboard-sided, two-story town hall that had been built sometime in the early 1920s. The below-ground atmosphere of neglected hygiene and guilty secrets gave her the creeps. She sometimes wondered if such oppressive surroundings might have had a psychological effect on her husband, on top of all the other dangerous, gruesome, and unsavory scenes that were part of his daily life. How could anyone keep his humanity, or his sanity, doing what he did and where he did it every day?

Descending a dozen worn stone steps to a basement entrance on the north side of Town Hall, she allowed her eyes to adjust to the dim indoor light before realizing that there was someone in the office. A young man dressed in the light grey uniform and black tie of a New York State Trooper sat at Joe's desk, tapping on the keyboard of Joe's computer. Bonnie approached and cleared her throat. "What are you doing?" she asked. The young man continued to tap away, his pale, smooth face fixed in the opened-mouth pose of a beagle on a chase. Bonnie raised her voice. "Sir, what are you doing here? This is my husband's office, and that's his computer."

The young man reached into his uniform shirt and retrieved a plastic badge. "BCI Forensic IT. Would you happen to know the password for this machine?"

"What? No."

The young trooper closed Joe's laptop and dropped it into a cloth bag marked 'EVIDENCE.' "S'all right. We can crack it at barracks." He picked up another bag, also marked 'EVIDENCE' and carried both toward the door.

"What are you taking?" Bonnie asked, pointing to the second bag.

"Can't say. Sorry."

But he didn't have to. From its shape, Luke's behavior, and a mother's unfailing instinct, she somehow knew that the bag marked 'EVIDENCE' contained a boy-sized hunting bow.

Chapter Five

Tom had arranged to meet with the German film distributor at his offices in the Old Town section of Baden-Baden, a picturesque spa town in the Black Forest where natural springs had been attracting wealthy visitors since the days of the Roman emperor Hadrian. Karlheinz Klopp was a gracious host and the suite he had arranged for Tom at the Brenners Park Hotel was palatial. He decided to walk from there to their morning meeting to organize his thoughts and review what he hoped to achieve during their short time together. Strolling through the public gardens along the Kurhaus Promenade, he was acutely aware of the meticulous attention to detail all around him, including a mile-long stretch of fitted stone block which covered the bottom of a mountain-fed stream that ran through the gardens and into the town. He reminded himself that Klopp would be equally well prepared, even if his agenda and wish list were unlikely to be revealed at this meeting. What Klopp might want in exchange for his box office data would be disclosed later. One of Tom's goals was to convince the German that later should be as soon as possible. A successful European film exchange would be a gold mine for everyone involved. But time was of the essence in assembling the necessary components. No one would make money if any of the key participants were tardy, recalcitrant, or greedy. That the film distributors might have to contribute capital, as well as data, was not something Tom intended to raise until later.

Arriving at Klopp's offices at the appointed hour, Tom was met at the door by the film distributor's personal assistant. Her English, attire, and even small talk, as she escorted him down a parquet hallway to Klopp's corner office, was flawless. Over rich pastries and watery coffee, the German began by noting that Klopp Enterprises had already built several pan-European businesses leveraging excess computer capacity from its core business. Tom had obviously gotten the idea for the film exchange from Klopp Enterprises.

He was right, of course. Though seeing where the German was heading, Tom took a moment to explain the principle of international intellectual property law that made Klopp's proprietary assertion unenforceable. "Ideas can't be owned, Karlheinz. Only the specific expression of them. No one has a protectable legal right to the idea of computer time-sharing."

Tom had been warned that Klopp didn't like to be contradicted in argument or anything else. But "you're stealing my idea" was a notion that had to be quickly squashed, if they were to spend their limited time on important details such as who does what, where, how, and for how much.

"Yes, yes," Klopp said. "Tell me more about this *expression* so my lawyers can tell me how you're ripping me off."

Tom summarized how a European film futures exchange would work, who would use it, and the ancillary services that would emerge to support its different product lines. Also, where he saw the money being made, how, and by whom.

"So, my idea."

"A piece of it, Karlheinz. With other pieces modeled from other industries. But the film exchange will be larger, more complex, and most importantly, more lucrative for anyone who gets in early and figures out where best to plant their stake. Being first with something that works is where the money will be made. Lots of it."

Klopp didn't respond at once. Instead, he told a humorous story about flying his friends, the Clintons, in his private airplane, hitting turbulence in the Alps, and watching Hillary leap voluntarily into her husband's lap, most likely for the first time in decades. Eventually, when he'd had sufficient time to sort his thoughts, he brought the conversation back to business.

"It will not be easy to do what you describe," said Klopp. "For historical reasons, media measurement remains politically sensitive in Germany. The politics require..." he paused, seeming to choose his English words carefully, "a sharing of benefits."

Tom didn't want to assume he knew precisely what Klopp meant by *sharing*. In New York, it might mean an obligatory campaign donation to both parties. In LA it might mean taking on an influential, but pain-in-the-ass silent partner. In Texas, a brown paper bag stuffed with cash was not entirely unknown. That's where Tom drew the line.

"I defer to you on local custom," Tom said. "But the exchange may burn through a lot of cash before it turns a profit. You should leave room at the trough for some other snouts in case we need them."

Klopp's pale, bushy eyebrows compressed into one. Tom clarified, "Additional investors."

"Yes, yes, of course. We will agree details later."

* * *

Bonnie called again just as Tom landed at Gatwick Airport. He didn't return her call. It wasn't that he was avoiding her. He simply couldn't think of anything to say that would not sound petulant. His decision not to rush to Joe's bedside was the right call. Joe didn't need his help, nor was it likely he wanted it. There was no longer any place for older brother in little brother's fiefdom.

And Bonnie and Mary had their own issues. Tom missed his nieces and nephew. He even missed his brother. His *little* brother. Not the big swinging dick that little brother had made himself into. As for their cold-as-an-Irish-kiss mother, her sudden hostility when Tom was last home struck him as irrational, even if she knew more than she'd admitted about the circumstances surrounding her husband's death. There could be any number of reasons why Joe had reacted so violently to Tom's pointed questions. But their mother's triumphant reaction to the outcome of her sons' physical confrontation made no sense. What had picking sides, or expressing unabashed satisfaction with the result, gained or spared her?

Tom closed his eyes and tried to bring order to his scattered thoughts. Harnessing a slippery character like Karlheinz Klopp should have been a satisfying challenge, and creating a new kind of financial market should have felt like an equally worthy undertaking. But he knew that creating a futures exchange to finance European films wasn't saving the planet. As maddening as his family could be, he missed them. Or, more accurately, the idea of a functional, loving family. The truth was that Morgans were a mess, and he had no idea of how to fix them. Joe was the undisputed king of Coldwater, Mary, the wrinkled hand behind the throne. When Tom pressed his tongue to the edge of his porcelain front teeth, he felt only sadness.

* * *

Tom slept lightly, waking more than once to the sounds of revelry in the street outside his flat. The neighborhood surrounding the lower Portobello Road was known primarily for its antique stores, weekend market, and other daytime distractions. Late-night carousing tended to center around the pubs near Notting Hill. But when the street performers elected to take advantage of the favorable acoustics near Market Square and succeeded in holding a sufficient crowd, the outdoor party could go on until the wee hours. Tom needed to be up early for a morning flight to Dublin. There, he hoped to convince a leading Irish software company to provide systems programming for the film exchange in exchange for a back-end fee instead of money upfront. The alternative was India. But he did not have time for the endless negotiation that New Delhi software firms seemed to relish.

Tom had always enjoyed doing business in Ireland. The Republic had revised its tax laws in the early 1980s to encourage foreign technology investment. Since then, and on account of its highly educated, English-speaking workforce, Dublin and its environs were the go-to place in Europe for the kind of data crunching that a European film futures exchange would require. He could have used the help of a tech-savvy legal associate for this part of the project. But Tanner had made it clear that the firm would not be providing additional resources. Tom was on his own for this part. And for everything else.

Ordinarily, it was no hardship to spend a day or more in the Irish capital.

Tom enjoyed the Irish people. They were friendly, outgoing, and, unlike their English cousins, what you saw was what you got. But there would be no time to enjoy the city and its sights on this trip. This was a check-the-box meeting and then back to the airport to catch a plane to Paris. There was much to be done, and the clock was ticking.

The technical part of the meeting with EmeraldSoft went well. As one of the principal data crunchers for the London Stock Exchange, they had the necessary capacity and expertise to meet most of the programming requirements for the film exchange. But they were candid that getting everything done by January 1st would be a problem, as would not getting paid up-front for their work. Tom asked the software development team to prepare a proposal of what they could do, when and for how much, and to be ready to present it in a week. Then he left for the airport and boarded a flight to Paris. He felt wired and tired.

Madame Huppe's driver met him at the Orly airport, and they rode in silence for the two-hour trip to Le Château Huppe. Tuning the car radio to the Paris Saint-Germain, Bayern Munich futbol match, the driver listened to the French take a drubbing from the Germans while Tom caught up on paperwork. Tom was not convinced that this get-to-know-you weekend was the best use of his time. If the idea of a European film futures exchange wasn't compelling enough on its own merits, how would a weekend of boozing and schmoozing change anyone's mind? Neither Karlheinz Kloop nor Madame Huppe had required much convincing. The need for an exchange was obvious and the arithmetic more than compelling. But he agreed that hopping from city to city for one-off dinners and breakfast meetings was inefficient. If *le weekend* went well, he hoped to have the three main European film distributors and their go-to exhibitors committed. Then he could turn his attention to the critical financial and product development pieces of putting the exchange together.

It was midnight when the car pulled up to a dark, *fin de siècle* country house fronted by a fountained formal garden and topped with a pillbox slate roof. The driver handed Tom's Gladstone bag to a uniformed *domestique* who led him up a central staircase where a dozen bedrooms lined two long hallways on either side of the second floor. Before falling asleep, he reviewed his notes on the production companies and exhibitors that he hoped to meet within the next two days. Then he took two Tylenol PM and crashed.

The following morning, before breakfast, he made a tour of the mansion's main floor and grounds. The interior space had been separated into a single wood-paneled great room on one side and diverse dining, kitchen, and occasional rooms on the other. Framed posters from the early days of French cinema, signed by the likes of Charlie Chaplin, Sarah Bernhardt, and Renée Adorée, decorated the main room as well as the attached smoking and card rooms. The floor plan was massive. Tom helped himself to a light breakfast from a sumptuous buffet that had been laid out in a far corner of the great room. Then he went outside for a run. He saw no other person until almost Noon.

While he had entertained a modest hope for the success of Madame Huppe's plan to combine business with pleasure, *le weekend* at Le Château Huppe turned out to be one of those cultural artifacts that was not likely to survive the decade. Before email, personal computers and cell phones, it may have been possible to bring people together in a place and manner that compelled them to focus exclusively on each other for a period sufficient to establish personal relationships. But the tether of unread emails and unplayed voicemails kept each of the guests umbilically connected to their laptops and mobile phones for most of the weekend. It wasn't until Sunday evening that Tom found himself in the same room with the three major European film distributors, released for the moment from their electronic overseers.

Entering the great room, he spotted Madame Huppe halfway across a vast expanse of oriental carpet, chatting with Karlheinz Klopp and Simon Fulton, the UK distributor. Elegant in a black Chanel evening dress and backlit by a blazing stone fireplace, she held out a glass of champagne in silent invitation for Tom to join the group. Karlheinz bared his sturdy teeth, Fulton frowned, and Madame Huppe slipped her arm through Tom's. "I give you Monsieur Thomas Morgan," she announced, "American financier, who claims that he can help the European film industry compete with Hollywood and produce higher quality film."

Fulton scoffed. "The highways are littered with skeletons of national film industries that have tried to compete with Hollywood. What makes Mr. Morgan think that his little financing gimmick will make any difference?"

"Tom?" asked Yvette.

Not knowing how long he might have the three distributors together, he kept his pitch short and, he hoped, convincing. "The European production companies have some of the best actors and directors in the world," he began. "But they don't have the capital to do special effects, quality outdoor sound, or large budget productions. The distributors and exhibitors show films one at a time in large theaters instead of showing multiple films in smaller venues, even though three-quarters of the seats in large theaters are empty and smaller theaters more profitable." He went on to explain how a European film futures exchange could provide the lower-cost capital necessary to fix these shortcomings.

When he was done, Madame Huppe spoke first. "Yes, yes. But we are already drowning in Hollywood trash. Why build tiny theaters to show *merde?"*

The UK distributor piled on. "How do we know that the production companies will use the cheaper funds to underwrite more and better films? How do we know that they won't use it to pay down debt, pump profits, or engage in some other financial sleight of hand? I'm sorry, Mr. Morgan, I don't see anyone in this room making a major capital investment in smaller theaters until we have enough quality product to fill the seats." Fulton's tone was bored, and his accent public school. Tom thought he might easily be mistaken for a banker instead of a film distributor.

"The exchange will provide capital to the European film industry at a lower cost than they can find anywhere else," Tom answered. "I don't claim to know how that money will be used, by who, or in what amounts. But given the time lag between production and distribution—sometimes years—any exhibitor that uses the cheaper capital to improve product, instead of fiddling with their balance sheet, will have a significant lead over any that don't. Enough of a lead that they might be difficult to catch."

Fulton scoffed. "Thank you for the business school primer. But, as you surely know, the City controls commercial financing in the UK. It's a clannish world. Do you have allies there? Need I tell you that Americans peddling exotic financial products are not popular? And that our banks have centuries of experience rolling logs at the feet of foreign interlopers who show up with fat checkbooks and little else?"

Tom smiled. *You're not going to be helpful, are you?*

"Then I suppose we're lucky that the exchange doesn't have to be located in London," Tom replied. "There are other European venues that might serve just as well."

"Brussels? Good luck."

"I was thinking more of Amsterdam. The Dutch take the long view, and they pride themselves in playing fair."

Yvette Huppe lifted a hand to cover her smile.

* * *

The following morning, Tom shared a car to the airport with a Monsieur Varné. Outside, the air was chill and the trees lining the country lane were bare of leaves. The driver cranked up the heat to semi-tropical, and Tom and his companion unbuttoned their jackets.

He assumed that Varné represented one of the smaller film distributors. They had not met or had a chance to speak over the weekend. But after a bit of chit-chat, the Frenchman explained that he was an "*entrepreneur internet.*" Then he went on to demonstrate a comprehensive grasp of everything Tom had said over the weekend. Varné pointed out several opportunities for the collection and sale of data other than box office—who's hot and who's not among the stars and directors, for example – and new internet services like MySpace and Friendster, where people join *les salles de conversation* to talk about common interests such as film. When Tom got a chance to break into the flood of ideas, he asked, "Would a film exchange need to put its own people in these chat rooms? That could be expensive and not very accurate."

"Perhaps there is a technology that could be used instead of people," Varné answered. "*La Sûreté* monitors the internet for terrorists, does it not? Perhaps the same technology could be used to listen to what people say about film actors and directors."

Tom found the idea intriguing, and the Frenchman refreshingly upbeat. He was a breath of fresh air after the recalcitrant distributors.

"Do you know anyone with contacts in the intelligence services?" Tom asked. "Or someone who could find out if any of the services might be willing to license their technology for commercial use?"

"I can make inquiries."

Tom liked the guy. Internet monitoring was not in the bare bones budget he had prepared for the initial launch. But Varné made an interesting case. "How much do you think this technology might cost?"

Varné spread his hands. "There is no precedent."

"Could you find out?"

"I can try."

"And if it's something the exchange could use, how would you be compensated?"

Varné tilted his head up and to the left. After a moment, he said, "I cannot find the English. A *prime de réussite?*"

"A success fee."

"*C'est ça*. The exchange would pay me only if we have the success."

* * *

Before boarding the plane to London, Tom put in a call to Tanner Hartwell. The distributors had been balky. But he was confident that they would make their data available to the film exchange once they were convinced it was viable. The next hurdle was obtaining the necessary funding to build the software systems and cover operating costs through a start-up period. The obvious source of funding was the law firm's client, as without the exchange, it had an embarrassing excess capacity problem and short-term financials that would torpedo its stock price. Tom could not understand why they would hesitate.

He waited several minutes for Tanner to come to the phone.

"I didn't get the answer you were hoping for," said Hartwell, as usual without preamble. "The chairman says that the company balance sheet won't support additional investment this quarter."

Abandoning his usual deferential tone, Tom scoffed, "That's a crock, Tanner. If the company doesn't pony up now, its next quarter will be a disaster."

Hartwell continued as if he hadn't heard, or it didn't matter. "And the chairman is still counting on a contract with the film exchange to be in place by the end of the year."

Tom struggled to maintain a respectful tone. "Does this guy understand that he'll be out of a job if he books that much income this quarter and then has to reverse it the next when his underfunded project doesn't get off the ground? The analysts will eviscerate him."

Hartwell took a moment to respond. "He's the client, Tom. He gets to call the shots. And he's been clear from the beginning that his company is only interested in unloading excess computer capacity for payment this quarter. You convinced him and the firm's management committee that it could be done. If that's no longer the case, then support for your project will have to end on January 1."

Tom got off the phone and walked across the terminal to the Air France Lounge. Taking a seat in a quiet corner overlooking the tarmac, he tried to sort out what had just happened and what it meant. *My project?*

You guys called me, remember?

Shit.

The firm would, of course, offer him space in its New York office, if the project ended. But then what? After nearly two decades of eighty-hour weeks working on other people's deals, he was no longer interested in the billable hours game, no matter how well-compensated. He'd made his pile, and he had already quit once—ignoring for the moment that the pile was almost completely invested in this film futures project. Before returning from his self-imposed retirement, he had decided that if he were to return to the game, it would be to work exclusively on his own deals—ones that created something useful, with a piece of the action for Tom Morgan. If after this, he had to work from someplace else or on his own, so be it. Though that assumed this project didn't implode and leave him penniless.

Shit.

But, if both the client and the firm bailed, was it realistic to think that he could still launch a successful film futures exchange without spending his last nickel and raising a lot more? Was there enough time? Always comfortable with risk, his strength was nevertheless complex project management, not high-stakes gambling. What were the odds that he could still complete the project without losing both his career and his capital? Slim? None?

Chapter Six

Joe descended the worn stone steps to the sheriff's office in the basement of Town Hall, aided by a decorative cane, a vial of Percodan, and a mummy's worth of restrictive bandaging around his midsection. It felt good to be upright and back on the job. What didn't feel good was finding a uniformed state trooper sitting behind MadDog's old desk, with his boot heels on the scarred oak and his big mouth yacking loudly into a landline. That the trooper was Joe's former deputy, Paulie Grogan, only added insult to trespass.

Grogan had left the Coldwater Sheriff's Department two years before in response to the NYS Bureau of Criminal Investigation's post-9/11 recruitment efforts in connection with the war on terrorism. The smarmy little shit had also taken Joe's two part-time deputies with him, leaving Joe with an unsustainable workload, tensions at home, and the mayor's disingenuous promise to staff up again "when the budget permitted."

Joe understood Bonnie's frustration at the sudden reduction of manpower in the Coldwater Sheriff's Department and the corresponding increase in her husband's workload and exposure to danger. But her expectation of what he could do about it was naive. Since their founding in 1917, the New York State Troopers had engaged in an ongoing battle with the small-town police and sheriff departments along the long water boundary with Canada over who was in charge and who was better able to keep a lid on the criminal element on either side. When MadDog was sheriff, he had won innumerable skirmishes in that long-running turf war by providing timely and often dramatic demonstrations that he was simply better at the task.

So, it was not surprising when after a few months on his new job, Paulie Grogan's position with the BCI turned out to have little to do with fighting terrorism. Or that the state trooper hierarchy simply used the extra budget and manpower to revisit its old objective of consolidating law enforcement along the maritime border with Quebec. Normally, Joe would not have been concerned with the territorial ambitions of his law enforcement rivals. The small-town police departments along the Quebec border had long and complex histories of live-and-let-live law enforcement with their Northern neighbors which gave them certain advantages. But after 9/11, nothing was ever going to be purely local again, and the grand prize in the control and consolidation game would remain, as it had always been, Coldwater.

Seeing his former deputy with his boots on the scarred wood of MadDog's old desk put Joe in a foul mood. He dropped a hand on the phone cradle and cut off the call. "You're in my chair."

Grogan didn't move. "You can't investigate your own shooting, Sheriff." The trooper gestured toward Joe's wooden cane. "And it doesn't look like you're fit for field work either."

"Is that what you're doing here? Fieldwork?" Joe closed his fist and held it at his side.

Grogan said nothing. But he didn't move.

"You've had ten guys out tramping the hillsides for a week with dogs and metal detectors," said Joe. "But all I hear they've found is a couple of rusty Skoal tins."

Grogan shot back. "And your blood near a tree stand, three hundred yards from where you said you were shot."

Joe looked at his former deputy, seemingly torn between yanking him to the floor or knocking some basic police procedure into his smarmy head. For a moment, the latter won out.

"That's right. I crawled from where I was shot to where I'd left my boy. That's what a dad does when there's an active shooter."

"But your boy wasn't there."

"No. You get skewered by an arrow; you let out a pretty good yell. Luke did what anyone would have—climbed out of the tree to find out what happened or get the hell away."

"But he didn't find you."

"He found the truck and stayed there like he was taught."

Grogan made a note on a leather-covered pad. "I'll need to talk to your son, Sheriff."

"Get out of my chair."

* * *

Grogan gathered his things and left. Joe waited a few minutes and then took the patrol car up the lake road to an unmarked dirt track known locally as Beaver Lane. Over the last few months, the sometimes lover's lane had become his favorite spot to sit and think in the afternoons. Nobody came there until after dark. It was private, and he had a lot to think about. But as he eased the patrol car down the rutted lane, it appeared that someone was there today. Under a canopy of white cedar, crowded by crushed oak fern, a blue Ford Taurus with a familiar license plate sat parked at the end of the dirt track facing the water.

Joe pulled the patrol car behind the Taurus and eased it forward until their bumpers kissed. Then he got out and knocked on the driver's side roof. The window descended slowly, and he leaned toward the woman inside. "Enjoying the mosquitoes, Mrs. Travis?"

"I always enjoy myself down here, Sheriff."

Maybe it had been a mistake to bring Crystal Travis to his private afternoon think spot. It seemed harmless at the time. Bonnie had been in Canada for seven months already, and it seemed unlikely that she would return anytime soon, if ever. He had only brought Mrs. Travis down here a few times, and not since Bonnie came back.

"You shouldn't come down here alone," he said, in a serious tone, "even in the daytime. Some wacko finds you, no one will hear the screams."

The dark-haired woman pressed a finger to an insect that was busy taking a blood sample from Joe's exposed forearm. "If you don't want to get bitten, Sheriff, the door on the other side is open." He looked toward the water and then back up the lane. *It's not like I go looking for this.* Bonnie had nothing to complain about. He had been doing the counseling and otherwise mostly behaving himself. But still, she took every opportunity to nag him about giving up his job as Coldwater Sheriff. Not directly. He'd been clear from the beginning that was a non-starter. But with a drip, drip, drip of pointed comment and observation. No opportunity missed. She knew or should have known that constant digs would not make him change his mind. What they did was wear out the goodwill he'd started with. Now, he was just annoyed.

A pair of mosquitoes landed in his ear and settled there like they'd found a new home. Crushing one and letting the other escape to find a new playmate, he looked toward the lagoon where he and the Dooley brothers had dodged bullets from that Fort Drum wackadoodle last year. Then he turned and gazed up the dirt track to where MadDog had gotten his throat cut all those years ago. *Life is short.*

Popping a Percodan, he shuffled to the other side of the Taurus, opened the door, and eased himself in.

* * *

The kids were asleep when Joe got home. Bonnie was up and waiting. "We've got to talk," she said as soon as he stepped inside the kitchen.

For a moment, Joe wondered if someone had spotted his patrol car or Crystal Travis's Taurus coming out of Beaver Lane. It seemed unlikely, but not impossible. "We've got that counselor tomorrow," he pointed out.

"Where I talk, and you say nothing."

Here we go.

"I say enough. Just not what you want me to." He watched her face become hard.

"You've nearly been killed three times in the past four years. But you act like it's nothing! As if the near certainty that you'll end up crippled or dead has no impact on me or our children! You don't talk about that, do you?"

He took a deep breath and struggled to keep his voice calm. "I didn't get shot on the job, Bonnie. I got shot on the opening day of deer season. Out in the woods with my son, like half the other dads in Coldwater. One of them got excited and mistook me for a deer, that's all."

"Opening day of archery season! You told me once that someone hunting with a bow and arrow had to get so close to its target, that it was impossible for them to mistake another human being for a deer."

"Guess I was wrong."

"Or you ran into some Coldwater lowlife with a score to settle."

Joe opened his mouth, thought better of it, and said nothing. He lowered his head and turned toward the door.

"Don't walk away from me!"

He turned with his hand on the doorknob. "We've been over this a thousand times, Bonnie. I don't have anything new to say. And obviously neither do you. So, I'm going to get some fresh air."

"Asshole."

Joe limped toward the tricked-out Silverado parked beside the shed at the far end of the gravel circle. Staring across ten acres of cleared land toward a lake half-lit by moonlight, he took a deep breath and then hoisted himself into the cab of the truck. "I don't need this shit." Then taking a moment to check his temper and catch his breath, he disengaged the brake and accelerated down the unpaved driveway, followed by a rooster tail of gravel and dust.

Bonnie returned to the house, scattering small stones with the toe of her shoe along the way. *Self-centered jerk!*

Inside, footsteps at the top of the stairs and a hastily closed bedroom door told her that someone had been listening. She thought of going upstairs to comfort whoever it was, thinking of the different tack she would have to take, depending on whether it was Luke or one of the girls. But she had no idea what she might say to any of them. *"Your father is a narcissist with a death wish? Or I've decided it would be better for all of us if..."* If what? Decided what?

Decided nothing. In the den, she retrieved a bottle of Smirnoff from the cabinet above the Kodiak gun safe and looked around for a glass. Feeling too weary to walk to the kitchen, she sat on the floor and began to sip from the half-empty bottle. Joe wasn't going to change. Which meant that nothing would. The truth was as simple and as maddening as that. What wasn't simple, was what to do about it.

The phone in her pocket that pressed against her pelvic bone reminded her that only a few months earlier she had taken a man's phone number and stored it in her phone while he watched and smiled hopefully. Why had she done that? Had she known then that she was going to leave Joe? Or that sooner or later she would have to, and that she would need help?

The man whose number she had taken was an old admirer from her high school days. Like many in Coldwater, he had relatives on both sides of the lake, and she ran into him a few times while she and the kids were staying with her parents. They'd gone out twice for a beer. He was a willing ear and she needed venting. Too, she had sensed that with a little encouragement, he might still be interested after all these years. The feeling was never mutual back in the day and it was not now. Though that didn't seem to discourage him. Mark Tremblay was no Joe Morgan. But she did not want another Joe Morgan. She wasn't sure she wanted anything. Peace and quiet, maybe. Financial stability, if possible. Safety for herself and her children, for sure. Yes, she needed that.

Feeling a familiar amalgam of anger, weariness, and defiance, she punched the number stored in her phone and waited. More confident that her old admirer would answer than she was sure that she wanted him to, she realized too that she had no idea what she would say when he answered.

Chapter Seven

The Percodan made Joe's head feel like Styrofoam. But he knew that he still needed the painkiller. He'd been lucky. An arrow through the lower torso that leaves only throbbing pain and stitches is a best-case scenario. A fuzzy head that interferes with thought and action is not. He'd been in and out of consciousness much of the time he was in the hospital. But he had sensed through whatever the doctors had given him that his mother was upset about something more than her son's skewering. He wasn't sure what was upsetting her. But experience counseled that it would be prudent to find out. Mary, with a bone in her teeth, could be a hurricane, especially if she wanted your attention and wasn't getting it.

Straddling the Silverado across a pair of parking spaces in front of Mary's condo, he thought briefly about popping another Percodan but decided against it. He might need his wits. He eased out of the truck and climbed the steps to the front door. It was his mother's geriatric admirer, Herbert, who answered his knock. "Glad to see you up and about, Sheriff."

"Hello, Mr. Ball. You're looking sharp this evening."

Herbert Ball had always reminded Joe of the aging Cary Grant. A little over six feet tall, lean, with a perpetual tan from his frequent visits to Florida and a full head of white hair that regularly sought the attention of an expensive barber. He almost always appeared in a tie and sport coat, with a trouser crease sharp enough to cut kindling.

Mary called from the couch. "Joseph, what are you doing out of bed?"

Joe noted the half-eaten plate of cheese and crackers on the coffee table and the nearly empty bottle of Sauvignon Blanc next to it. "Looks like I'm crashing a party."

Herbert smiled. Mary didn't. "You're not in uniform. You didn't call ahead, and it's after ten o'clock. Why are you here? What's wrong?"

I'm here to find out why I'm here, would have been an honest answer. But his brain felt too slow to risk candor. *Goddamn drugs.* After a moment of uncomfortable silence, he muttered, "I'll come by in the morning."

Mary looked at him hard. "Yes. We need to talk."

Okay. Thought so.

Herbert, who had just eased back into the soft chair next to the couch, heaved himself upright and accompanied Joe to the door. "Your mother's right. You should be in bed. You look exhausted. I can't imagine how you get in and out of that outsized vehicle with your injury."

"Drugs."

Herbert reached into his pocket and removed a set of car keys attached to a monogrammed gold fob. "Take the Buick. It's easier to get in and out of. You can bring it back tomorrow when you come to see your mother."

Joe nodded. "Good idea, thanks." He took the Buick keys and handed the Silverado key to Herbert. "In case you need to move it."

Herbert pocketed the key. "Spend some time with your mother, if you can. She's a bit edgy about something."

"Anything in particular?"

"You, I imagine."

* * *

Joe left his mother's apartment and found the Buick parked at the opposite end of the condominium lot. As advertised, the Buick was a lot easier to get into than the Silverado. Though, it would probably drive like the living room. After adjusting the unfamiliar seat and surveying the fancy dashboard knobs and buttons, Joe looked toward the hills above town and at the stars flickering in the clear, cold air above them. Going home didn't seem like a good idea. Bonnie would still be up. He didn't have the energy or interest in more confrontation. Spending the night on the couch in the sheriff's office didn't appeal either. Looking toward town, he reached into his pocket and absently rolled the vial of pain pills between thumb and fingers. Crystal Travis had made a point of mentioning that her truck-driving husband was on the road this week. The invitation was clear. Going there was arguably better than going home or spending an uncomfortable night on a lumpy couch in the sheriff's office.

After rolling down the car window and cranking up the FM radio, he turned the geezermobile in the direction his drug-numbed brain had chosen as his best option, and didn't give the decision any more thought after that.

* * *

"She's going to take my grandchildren." Mary lifted her glass of white wine and drained what was left of it.

Herbert knew better than to object, though some response seemed called for. "I thought they were seeing a marriage counselor," he said.

"There's no compromise in that girl. And no *umph* in her husband all of a sudden."

"Mary, he was just shot."

"My point. And hers, too, unfortunately. If Joseph doesn't pull himself together, he's going to wake up to an empty house. And that will be the last I'll see of my grandchildren." Mary reached to refill her glass and saw that the bottle was empty. "I don't know why you gave him your car keys. Can you drive that thing he left outside?"

"If need be."

"Need be," she grimaced.

He found a footstool in the kitchen, and they used it to climb into the jacked-up Silverado, both grateful that it wasn't a stick shift. Driving carefully, he turned the truck in the direction of town while Mary continued to fret aloud. He tried to concentrate on what she was saying and to make suitable comments, all the while wrestling with a steering wheel the size of a lazy Susan and unfamiliar heat controls. Then, as they approached a long stretch of curved road, a large vehicle in serious need of muffler repair pulled up behind them and flooded the Silverado with bright, halogen light that lit up the interior of the truck like a nighttime bombardment. Herbert looked for the button, or whatever, to lower the window and signal the idiot to pass.

"What's going on?" asked Mary.

"I don't know. Some punk in a hurry." Herbert found what he was looking for, lowered the window, and stuck out his arm, moving it clockwise in the universal hand signal for "pass." The vehicle behind them responded by accelerating and ramming the Silverado hard from behind.

Mary let out a noise like a small, surprised animal. Herbert lurched forward into his shoulder belt and stomped on the brake. The vehicle behind them accelerated and rammed into them again. The Silverado veered toward a ditch.

"What's going on?" Mary's voice sounded surprisingly calm under the circumstances.

"I don't know. But you'd better hold on to something." Herbert shifted from brake to accelerator and tried to keep the unfamiliar Silverado in the center of the road. The trailing vehicle accelerated and crashed into them twice more.

Then Herbert felt his chest tighten. The lights of the town sparkled a mile away. Struggling to keep the outsized vehicle in the center of the road, he felt a sharp pain shoot up his left arm. Mary said something he couldn't understand, unbuckled her seat belt, and grabbed the steering wheel. Another hard ram from behind, followed by an accelerated push, drove the Silverado off the road and into a steep ravine. Halfway down, it overturned, rolled twice, skidded on its roof, and came to rest nose-down in a muck-filled ditch. The last thing Herbert felt was the taste of stagnant water.

* * *

Bonnie pulled into the parking lot of Trudy's Diner, a converted 1950s-era aluminum Airstream with half a dozen bench booths beside a row of dust-caked windows that looked out over a gravel parking lot. Mark Tremblay had arrived early and was sitting in the back booth farthest from the door.

Bonnie turned off the car engine and placed her hands on top of the steering wheel and her forehead on top of her hands. *Are you ready for this?*

Ready for what? To do what? Say what? She had no idea. No plan. All she knew was that she and her children had run out of options. Resting her head on the steering wheel, with only the sound of her own shallow breath to mark time, she made up her mind to go into the diner and let whatever was about to happen, happen. Mark's eyes were on her as she came through the door and made her way toward the booth where he sat. He stood while she settled into the bench seat opposite.

"I was surprised to get your phone call," he said while she slipped off her coat and arranged it on the bench beside her. "Pleased, but surprised. I was afraid that you might have forgotten me."

She smiled weakly. "Thanks for coming, Mark. I didn't know who else to call."

"Has something happened?"

She took a deep breath and held his gaze. "I'm leaving Joe." Until the words came out, she had not known what she was going to say, or that she'd actually made up her mind. But once out, everything that followed seemed to flow as a matter of course. "I mean, I've *decided* to leave him," she said. "But I haven't done it. I'm not sure…" It took her several tries and minutes to explain the compelling whys and seemingly impossible hows. She knew that she needed to leave. There wasn't ever going to be a better time. But she feared jumping into the unknown might just be going from the frying pan into the fire. She had no resources, no place to go, three kids who wouldn't want to go and who, in every material way, would be worse off if and when she did. And who knew what Joe would do?

Tremblay listened and did not interrupt. When Bonnie finished speaking, he let the silence linger before asking, "How can I help?"

"I don't know, Mark. I don't even know why I called you. I mean, you're already helping me just by listening. I guess I need… I don't know, a reality check. I need to make sure I'm not crazy. I keep thinking about that Paul Simon song, *There Must Be Fifty Ways To Leave Your Lover.* What a crock!"

Tremblay reached his hands across the Formica table. Bonnie kept hers folded in her lap. "Are you safe?" he asked.

Bonnie raised her shoulders. "I guess. I don't know. Joe's never been violent at home."

Tremblay drew his hands back. "Well, the concerns you mentioned are real enough. But they're not going to come down on you all at once unless you throw the kids in the back of the car and peel out of the driveway three steps ahead of the madman. You've got time. You can manage it without jumping straight into poverty and homelessness."

"How?"

"By getting a lawyer. By going after temporary child support so you can put food on the table while the process runs its course. Every woman I've ever heard of in your situation who has kids got to stay in the house. At least until the divorce was final. You shouldn't have to worry about a place to stay."

"Joe will never move out."

"Talk to a lawyer, Bonnie. They get paid to work this stuff out."

"I can't afford one, Mark."

"You don't know that, Bonnie. I'm sure there's a lawyer in town who would do it on a contingency, or whatever it's called."

Bonnie put a hand to her forehead. Tremblay raised his to catch the attention of the waitress. "Have you eaten?"

"No. Yes. Maybe just coffee."

When the waitress came over, Tremblay ordered two coffees and a slice of pumpkin pie. Then he leaned across the table and placed his hands just over the center. "You've done the hard part. Making the decision. But, to get what you need for you and the children, you need a lawyer."

"I don't know, Mark."

"Sure you do, or you wouldn't be here. Calling me was a big step. You know how I feel."

Bonnie closed her eyes. "I just need a friend right now, Mark. That's all I can handle."

Tremblay held up his hand. "Of course."

The waitress brought the coffee and pie. Tremblay ate in silence while

Bonnie sipped her coffee. When he finished, he pushed the plate to one side and continued. "Do you remember my sister, Bernadette? She still lives here in town. But a few years ago, she got divorced. Her lawyer's name is BeauSoleil, and he's got offices on both sides of the lake. That could be useful if you decide not to stay in Coldwater."

"I don't know..."

"It can't hurt to talk. He might put some of your fears to rest."

"Joe will freak."

"But you'll '*get yourself free*.'"

* * *

It was late by the time Bonnie got home from her tête à tête with Mark Tremblay. She went straight to bed, slept badly, and got up early to make breakfast for the kids. As she was scrambling eggs, a state trooper's car came up the gravel driveway and stopped in front of the house. She looked past it to the shed where Joe's truck should have been. Of course, it wasn't there. The trooper who got out of the car and walked toward the kitchen door was Paulie Grogan.

"Is the sheriff home?" he asked when Bonnie opened the door.

"Good morning, Paulie. I don't see his truck. He must have left early."

"Have you seen him this morning?"

Bonnie felt her face tighten. "I'm afraid not."

"Would you mind calling him?"

She wiped her hands on the dishcloth that she had carried to the door. "Is there something wrong, Paulie?"

"There's been an accident."

She felt her stomach flip.

"Not your husband, Mrs. Morgan. His vehicle. But I need to speak with him. Maybe if you call him, he'll pick up."

Bonnie gestured toward the kitchen. "Come inside. Please." Grogan followed and waited while Bonnie picked up the kitchen wall phone, dialed her husband's number, and got his voicemail. "Joe, Paulie Grogan is here.

He says that there's been an accident involving your truck. Please call him when you get this."

Meghan and Kate came into the kitchen. "Hi, Mr. Grogan," said Kate.

Grogan nodded. "Mrs. Morgan, can we step outside?" Bonnie told the girls to make toast and then followed Grogan outside. "I'm sorry to bring you news like this," he said. "But since I haven't been able to get through to the sheriff, I need to tell you that your mother-in-law and a man named Herbert Ball were in an accident sometime late last night or early this morning. It appears that Mr. Ball may have suffered a heart attack while driving your husband's truck. Your mother-in-law was a passenger in it, and both she and Mr. Ball were killed."

Bonnie felt her heart clench. "Dear God."

Chapter Eight

It was mid-afternoon in London when Tom's phone started to light up with calls from his sister-in-law. He let them go to voice mail. It was Father Gauss who finally got through to him. The priest gave Tom what information he had. His mother had been a passenger in a car that went off the road when the driver suffered a heart attack. She and the driver were killed. "I'm sorry, Tom. Stop by the rectory when you get to town. I may have more information by then."

Tom had been reasonably prepared for MadDog's death, having witnessed his parents' frequent arguments over the dangers of his father's job. So, when in Tom's final year of law school, Joe called with the news that their father's body had been found in the front seat of his patrol car with his throat cut open from side-to-side, it came as a shock, but not a surprise. Though, it was both when Morini's Funeral Home discovered stacks of one hundred dollar bills stuffed into the lining of the suit coat that Mary had provided for her husband to be buried in.

Most boys are imprinted by their fathers. But when yours wears a uniform and carries a gun, impressions can be as deeply ingrained as a tattoo. When the end came for MadDog, the surprise was not that he had died with his boots on, so to speak, but that the larger-than-life father of Tom's melancholy childhood had been just another cop on the take.

Mary's sudden death was a different kind of shock. Women like her were forces of nature who exuded the self-possession of a life not easily ended. Though somehow it had. Now, Tom found himself asking the kinds of questions that he had never had the courage or inclination to ask before.

Who was my mother? What made her tick? And what had made her the prickly, iron-willed enigma that he had never come close to understanding? On the seven-and-a-half-hour flight to Montreal, he tried to come up with answers.

His mother had not been a happy person. The lens through which she viewed the world primarily focused on trouble: world and local tragedy, what might be coming down the road in her own life and that of her family, and what had already arrived and needed to be fixed or endured. Her conversation had been equal parts criticism and command. Only the grandchildren escaped her constant efforts to orchestrate everything in her immediate environment, and then only because Bonnie would not tolerate interference with her own parental prerogatives. But the grandchildren remained a constant focus of worry. Mary had been angry when Bonnie took them to Canada and agitated until she brought them back. But if she had felt joy or happiness when the grandchildren returned, Tom had seen no evidence of it.

Why had his mother been the way she was – demanding, bossy, alternatively hot-tempered and dismissively cold? And what, if anything, might explain her partisan cheerleading to near fratricide that had concluded Tom's last visit to Coldwater? Had his renewed inquiries into the death of her husband threatened the carefully constructed facade of '*la famille* Morgan?' Would the answers have further undermined the fiction that MadDog had been an honest cop and faithful husband? Or the lie that he had been a hero protector to his community, tragically killed on the job? That his son, heir, and latest badass Sheriff Morgan was an upstanding pillar of the community, too? Was there anyone in Coldwater who still believed any of that?

Tom's refusal to accept the family fairy tale had been an uncomfortable mirror of truth to them all. Though, the family folded him easily back into the myth once he'd left. Peddling the tale of the brainiac child who'd gone off to conquer the world, it worked as long as he stayed away from Coldwater and only came back on occasion. But on his last visit, he got dragged into helping Joe investigate the death of Dee Dee Ryan. And that led to some hard-to-avoid questions about MadDog's still unsolved murder. All hell broke loose then. But why? Would have discovering who killed MadDog and why put *finis* to the family lie of heroic achievement? And if it did, so what? Had preserving the fantasy been more important to Mary than creating an honest and loving environment that might have kept her family healthy and intact?

What did he really know about his mother, other than that she was chronically unhappy and, at times, inexplicably vicious? He knew she was distantly related to the Hellers, an extended clan of violent Coldwater criminals. Though she would never admit it. He knew, too, that she was possessed of a ferocious temper, though she suffered a philandering husband without retribution and expected Bonnie to do the same. Or had she? It was that line of inquiry that had gotten Tom a new set of front teeth.

Which told him what?

Tom asked the steward for a cup of coffee and sipped it while he gazed out the porthole window at a moonlit carpet of clouds. Did *any* of these questions have a discoverable answer? Did the answers matter? With Mary dead, who was his family now? Joe, who seemed to be turning by degrees into an even more violent version of their notoriously violent father? Bonnie, who was failing in her effort to turn her husband into something he did not want to be and facing the consequences of becoming the next generation of look-the-other-way Morgan spouses. Were his nieces and nephew his family? Is home wherever the kids are? And if Bonnie failed to turn Joe around, which seemed likely, what would become of the Morgan 'family' then? What useful role, if any, would there then be for the outcast Uncle Tom?

The answers were obvious as well as sad. Unless someone or something succeeded in stopping Joe's determined march toward self-destruction, the Morgan family would scatter. Bonnie would move on. And Luke? What would become of Tom's fishing buddy? Would he see his nephew again? The girls would be teenagers soon, disappearing into that long, dark tunnel where almost anything might happen. Will you be there for that, Joe? Or will Bonnie and your kids be gone and far away? And if gone, are you still the cock of Coldwater, Sheriff Joe Morgan? Or, like MadDog, are you pushing up daisies?

Any way Tom looked at it, the future seemed grim.

* * *

It took less than an hour for Tom to get through customs at the Montreal-Trudeau airport and less than that to rent a car and drive over the border to Coldwater. Ease of entry was one of the reasons he preferred to fly into Montreal-Trudeau instead of JFK when he came to the States and had time to stop in Coldwater. Another was that it gave him time to ease back into the rural culture and pace of the little towns that dotted the long land and water border with Quebec.

Entering Coldwater from the north, he drove the lake road lost in thought, past rows of gabled houses and vistas of blue water that sparkled in the morning sunlight. Then he left the car by the side of the road and climbed a set of worn stone steps to a three-story wooden structure that hadn't seen fresh paint in decades. He pressed a familiar tinny-sounding bell, and after a suitable delay, a pear-shaped figure topped with a braided white bun appeared at the door.

"Hello, Mrs. Flynn."

"I'm sorry for your troubles," she said simply. "He's in his study."

At the end of a dark, airless hallway, he entered a room lined on three sides by floor-to-ceiling bookshelves and on the fourth, which faced the lake, by a long row of single-pane windows. The windows were original and poorly maintained, swelling shut in summer and leaking frigid drafts of cold northern air in winter, which a trio of electric floor heaters could never quite overcome. It was in this room that a young Tommy Morgan had first discovered that he had a brain and had later spent many a challenging hour with the man who taught him to use it. Father Gauss was seated that morning in his usual spot behind the antique trestle table that served as his desk, writing something in long hand with a Parker fountain pen. The priest refused to compose at a computer, having once told Tom that the ease of correction made his sermons too wordy.

"I'm sorry," said Gauss looking up from his writing. He stepped out from behind his desk and walked over to Tom, wrapping an arm around his shoulders. Tom felt the tension he had been holding seep into the scarred wooden floor. Mrs. Flynn appeared with a tray of coffee and scones and left them on a corner of the table.

"Any news?" Tom asked when the housekeeper had left the room.

"I'm afraid not," said Gauss. "I've only spoken with your brother's wife, and we've only spoken about arrangements for the funeral. It's tomorrow, by the way. 10:00 am."

"That's quick, isn't it?"

The priest made an equivocal gesture.

"What about the driver, Herbert Ball?"

"I'm told he had a heart attack. Also, that there has been some difficulty locating next of kin."

Tom frowned. "That's not often a problem with rich guys, is it?"

Gauss spread his hands again.

"What about my brother? Has he figured out yet who slipped an arrow through his ribs?"

Gauss gave Tom a long, assessing look. "I'm told that the state troopers have taken over the investigation."

"He must be spitting."

Gauss filled the two coffee mugs and handed one to Tom. "Never mind your brother and Mr. Ball for the moment. Tell me something happy about your mother. I need to prepare remarks for the service tomorrow. A favorite childhood memory would be nice."

Tom looked through the ripple-paned windows at a line of choppy waves pushing south across Wilson Cove. "I'm sorry, Father. I don't have any of those. My mother was not a happy woman. I've just spent seven and a half hours on a plane trying to figure out why."

"Did she make others happy?"

"Not intentionally."

The priest sighed. "We're all flawed, Tommy. Your mother was no exception. But tomorrow, we celebrate the life of a fellow human being."

Unwilling to surrender to false sentimentality, Tom responded. "Who may or may not have been involved in the death of her husband. Who applauded her younger son's rise to the hotly contested title of most violent law enforcement officer on either side of Coldwater Lake, and who openly celebrated this." He crooked a finger in the direction of his new porcelain front teeth.

Gauss stared into his cup of coffee as if waiting for a sign. "Let me try this another way. How's your soul?"

Tom held his forehead in his hand. "I can't go there, Father."

The priest glanced at the row of lake-facing windows and then walked to the wall of books opposite. "We've known each other since you were eleven years old," he said, staring up at the shelves of books. "In fact, you're older now than I was when I first came to Coldwater."

Tom forced a short laugh. "Why do people feel seemed compelled lately to remind me of how long I've been on this planet? Coupled with how little I've accomplished."

Gauss ignored the complaint and pushed a set of library steps into a corner of the room. Then he climbed until he was standing eye to eye with the top third of shelving. "Most of the wisdom traditions come out, more or less, at the same place," he said from the height. "Sublimation of the ego and service to others. I've been spoon and force-feeding different ones to you for the better part of three decades, hoping that sooner or later, you'd find one that fits you better than the one you were born into. But now I think that I may have been taking the wrong approach." He ran his hand across a row of titles. "Tommy Morgan may not be designed to fit into any of them. But maybe he's meant to discover one."

The priest reached toward the third shelf from the top and took down two thin, leather-bound volumes. One he dropped in Tom's lap, and the other he held onto as he made his way back to the cracked leather chair behind the trestle table.

"*The Apologia*?" Tom asked, tilting his head to read the embossed title. "We read this together when I was in high school."

"Yes. Well, I may have brought out the big guns too soon," Gauss grumbled.

"Do you remember any of it?"

"Plato's account of Socrates giving his judges a piece of his mind and speculating about life after death."

"Do you remember him talking about his guardian angel?"

"No. That's Christian cosmology, isn't it? Not ancient Greek."

"Well, the term Plato used was *daimon*. The church picked it up around the fourth century and turned it into a guardian angel. But the idea is the same. A non-corporeal, spiritual being assigned to each human at birth whose purpose is to kick their assignee's ass whenever he or she strays from *the path*. The church's version became a small voice that's supposed to whisper in your ear when you're contemplating something sinful. The original Greek version was much broader and a lot harsher."

Tom settled into his chair. This was the part of his old mentor that he deeply admired and often missed.

"The Greek *daimon* doesn't just admonish," Gauss continued. "It actively interferes. And the path that the *daimon* is supposed to make sure its human follows is not the road to heaven. It's an earthly path that's intended to lead the *daimon*'s human to become whomever he or she is uniquely meant to be."

"A conscience you can't ignore?"

"More than that. The *daimon* has no scruples about causing trouble designed to persuade its human to find or stay on that human's *unique* path. Something like a *djinn* in that respect." Gauss handed Tom the other slim volume. "What do you remember of this one?"

Tom ran his finger over the gold leaf lettering: *The Republic*. "Plato's theory of form, the story of the cave. Not much about his *ideal state*. Fascism didn't hold much interest for me then, or now."

"Good enough. You remember Plato's idea that there's an ideal *form* that captures the essence of everything? If it's got four wheels and an engine, it's a car, no matter the variation. Three legs and a seat, it's a stool, and so forth. Plato looked for the general in the specific. But he never turned the lens around to look the other way around."

"And if he had?"

"That's what I want you to find out."

"You want me to take on Plato? Now?"

"Only if you're tired of torched houses, busted romances and, let me guess, choppy sailing on whatever it is you're up to now. I'd say your guardian angel/daimon has been opening doors and lighting fires under your butt ever since we first met. In fact, I'm sure that's why we met. But since you haven't yet figured out what you're ignoring or straying from, your daimon/guardian angel has continued to make your life strategically miserable. Has it not?"

Tom snorted. "Don't take me wrong, Father. But do your people still burn heretics at the stake?"

"This isn't heresy, Tommy. I'm just giving your guardian angel credit for doing more than keeping little Tommy Morgan from impure thoughts. If the church is going to borrow from the Greeks, it should at least have the humility to get it right."

Tom opened the leather volumes and flipped through their pages. "You think the *answer* to what Tom Morgan is supposed to do with his life is in here?"

"I have no idea. To be honest, I'm almost out of ideas. But it never hurts to read and think."

Tom remained silent. Gauss pressed the point. "If you re-frame Plato's idea of the *form,* looking for the specific rather than the general, there must be a *form* called Tommy Morgan who can't be anyone else other than whom he was meant to be. If Socrates and the church are right, your daimon/guardian angel has been opening doors and lighting fires under your butt since you were born, all in an effort to keep you on the path to where and what you're uniquely supposed to be. And fair warning: daimons/guardian angels are immortal. They don't give up. Until you recognize the doors that yours has been opening and walk through them, you're going to continue to suffer some serious burnt-ass syndrome. For the rest of your life, if necessary."

Mrs. Flynn chose that moment to reappear at the door wearing an apologetic look. "It's Bishop Mczynski's office on the phone. I told them you were busy, but they said it was urgent."

Gauss came around to the front of the desk. "Stop by again before you leave town if you have time." Tom held out his hand. The priest took it and added a one-armed hug. "You've been my most challenging project for as long as I can remember, Tommy Morgan."

"And you're not even my *daimon*."

Chapter Nine

W*ho was my mother? What made her tick? Had she ever been happy?*

Tom could think of only one person who might have an answer to the mystery of Mary Morgan: her friend of fifty years and Tom's junior high school science teacher, Rosemary Ryan. Whether Mrs. Ryan would agree to talk with him was another question. Given their last communication, she was more likely to turn a hose on her former pupil and then slam a door in his face.

Tom drove the rental car south toward town, turning right at the statue of Revolutionary War heroine, Sybil Ludington, then ascending the steep, single-lane road that divided the east and west sides of Wilson Point. Halfway up, he stopped at the top of a nearly vertical driveway and set the car's emergency brake, placing a pair of paving blocks left there for that purpose behind the car's rear tires. Then he stepped cautiously down the slick, half-moon driveway toward the clapboard cottage perched high over the lake, and waited there outside the kitchen door for someone to answer his knock.

Rosemary Ryan typically spent the summer here in the home of her banker son, Andrew. While she had likely returned to Florida several weeks ago, Tom hoped that she might have returned to Coldwater for her old friend's funeral and, on account of the somber circumstances, that she might be willing to talk to him.

His last communication with Mrs. Ryan had been shortly before his exile from Coldwater, delivered in the form of a church bulletin wrapped around a crumpled protein bar wrapper. The not-so-subtle message had been intended to let his old teacher know that her former pupil had figured out her role in the drowning death of her daughter-in-law, Dee Dee. He had always intended to keep his old teacher's secret, and he had. The death had obviously been unintentional. But he had wanted to let her know that he knew. Hubris?

Tom would not have been surprised if Rosemary Ryan dumped a pail of slop from an upstairs window, or more likely, just left him standing outside indefinitely. But if she was here, he hoped that she would speak with him. There was no one else likely to have the answers he was looking for.

While he waited for someone to answer his knock, his thoughts turned toward Mrs. Ryan's granddaughter, Maggie, an attractive, porcelain-skinned brunette who he had met on his last visit to Coldwater. As many years his junior as Yvette Huppe was his senior, Miss Ryan had recently accepted a job teaching first grade at Our Lady of The Lake Elementary School. Father Gauss, her nominal employer, had asked Tom to befriend his newest teacher but refrain from becoming romantically involved. "You're too old," he'd said bluntly. "But a platonic friendship with someone who had also yet to figure out what he was meant to do with his life might be of some use to Miss Ryan. She's not meant to be a teacher."

Tom had found the befriending part enjoyable. The *refraining* part, not so much.

After several long minutes, the side door to the Ryan kitchen opened and Mrs. Ryan's middle-aged son, Andrew, father of Maggie, filled the doorway. His expression combined surprise and wariness, though it quickly morphed into an appropriate frown of condolence. "Hello, Tom," he said. "I'm sorry for your troubles."

"Hello, Andrew. May I come in?"

"Of course." Ryan opened the door just wide enough for Tom to step inside. "Maggie isn't here, I'm afraid," he said. "She's taking art classes in Amsterdam."

"How is she?"

Ryan smirked. "Doing well, I suppose. I'd know more if she'd call or write. But my mother is here. The weather's been so nice this fall, she hasn't headed back to Florida yet. I'm sure she'd be happy to see you."

Tom questioned the prediction of welcome. But he smiled politely. "I was hoping Mrs. Ryan would be here. Our mothers were close friends, and I have a few questions that she might be able to help me with."

Andrew nodded. "Of course. Why don't you wait on the sun porch? You know the way. I'll let Mother know you're here."

Tom exited the kitchen and passed through a room filled with easy chairs and couches, low bookshelves, and a tall stone fireplace. On the east-facing sun porch, he made himself comfortable on flower-patterned cushions and waited for his old teacher to come downstairs. He still wasn't sure exactly what he was going to ask her. Who was my mother? Why was she such a cold, unhappy Stoic? Was it nature, or was there a story? He would have to come up with something.

Lost in musing, it was a moment before he noticed his old teacher standing silently in the doorway, an undisguised frown covering the bottom half of her face. She had pulled her hair back in a short, white ponytail and had dressed in an ankle-length pleated white skirt, patterned blouse, and tan vest. Mrs. Ryan may have had to pull herself together in a hurry, but she had come down to face her former student in her prim, schoolmarm best. Tom stood, but he did not offer a hand. "Thank you for seeing me, Mrs. Ryan."

Rosemary remained standing, making no move to either enter the room or sit down. "My son says you have some questions about your mother."

"If you'll indulge me."

"I didn't much care for our last conversation, Thomas," she said, referring to his effort to help Joe investigate the drowning death of Andrew Ryan's second wife, Dee Dee, by asking Rosemary about a rumored affair between his first wife and the deceased Sheriff Morgan. His old teacher had refused to answer any of his questions, though he ultimately found what he needed elsewhere. He hoped that his mother's old friend might be more forthcoming today, as there was unlikely an elsewhere for this particular inquiry.

"I've just come from visiting our mutual friend, Father Gauss," he began. "My mother's funeral is tomorrow, and Father Gauss asked me to share some happy memories of her that might help him prepare his remarks for the service. I had to confess that I don't have any."

He paused, but Rosemary declined to fill the gap.

"We both know that my mother was not a happy person. But other than the fact that she was married to a violent, alcoholic, misogynistic philanderer, I have no idea why."

Rosemary remained silent.

"You're a bright woman, Mrs. Ryan," Tom prompted. "You don't miss much. And you and my mother were friends for more than fifty years."

Rosemary stared out the porch window for half a minute before finally entering the room and taking a seat on one of the rattan chairs opposite the couch. But she continued to frown and say nothing.

Just spit it out.

"What I'd like to know is this," said Tom. "Was my mother ever happy? And if so, what happened to change that?"

Rosemary shifted her weight on the green flowered cushions and simultaneously frowned. "Why do you want to know, Thomas? And why now?"

It was a fair question. And he wasn't sure that he fully understood his own motivations. He began with a simple, "Because she was my mother. Because her story is the foundation of mine and my brother's. Because it's a poorly understood piece of how we're both turning out. And because waiting for her to finally spill the beans is no longer an option."

Rosemary continued to frown. "Suppose your mother didn't want you to know? My friend was a very private woman."

"And so is your son's first wife, Karen," said Tom. "But your granddaughter, Maggie, would have suffered needlessly had you and Andrew put her biological mother's privacy ahead of Maggie's doctors' need to know her family medical history."

Rosemary sat upright and stared out at the lake through rain-spotted windows. "You make a good argument," she said at last. "Not surprisingly."

He waited.

"Alright, then. Your mother was happy when we were girls. Not especially happy. Just normal girl happy. Giggles and fun."

He waited for more. But when he realized that Rosemary deemed her answer sufficient, he prompted. "When did that change? And why, if you know?"

Rosemary continued to stare out the lake-facing window, seemingly reluctant to meet her interrogator's gaze. But at last, she said. "After high school." She paused and then added, "Your mother had a good time there. She was outgoing. A bit of a wild woman, actually. She knew how to have fun."

"Did that change when she married my father?"

Rosemary shook her head. "No. It was before that. After her "Big Adventure," as she called it. After she went to New York and then came home."

Tom was surprised. "I never knew that my mother had *ever* left Coldwater, except for that one time she and MadDog went to Florida."

Rosemary gave him a sharp look. "Be respectful, Thomas."

He dropped his head.

"The Big Adventure didn't last long." she continued. "Your grandfather had been after your mother to get married right after high school when she was dating your father the first time. He told her that if she didn't settle down soon, she'd be an old maid and that she had to get out of the house. Your mother didn't want to settle down. She wanted to taste life. So, she broke off the relationship with your father, took a bus to New York, got a job in a law firm, and went off to have what she called her *Adventure*."

"What brought her back to Coldwater?"

His old teacher's eyes were cold and unsympathetic. "She got pregnant."

Tom took a short, sharp breath.

"She didn't tell anybody, of course. She just came home and did what she had to do: make up with your father and get him to propose."

"Did MadDog know?"

Rosemary glared. "Enough of that. His name was the same as yours. And no, of course, he didn't. Though over time, he may have come to suspect."

"I see."

"Do you? I don't see how any man of your generation could possibly imagine what it was like to have been an unmarried girl *in the family way* back then. Your grandfather would have killed your mother if he'd found out. I mean that literally. Mary was in a desperate situation, with the clock ticking. 'He's the best catch in town," she said to me after she'd gotten your father to propose. 'Too bad it's not much of a town."

Tom lifted his head and looked toward the lake. "That's so sad."

"For everyone," Rosemary agreed, "for her, for your father. The unacknowledged and always present must have been unbearable at times. Your mother met her wifely and motherly duties as she saw them. But over time, she became bitter and resentful."

Tom folded his hands and stared at the ring marks that stained the glass-topped coffee table. *Well, that explains a lot.*

"So MadDog was not my father."

Rosemary glared again but nodded sharply.

"I can't say I'm displeased. Did my mother ever say who my father was?"

"No," said Rosemary, in a tone that made Tom uncertain whether she was telling the truth. "She said he was married, of course. That he was some big-shot Manhattan lawyer. And that I would recognize his name if she told me. But she never did, and I didn't ask."

* * *

So MadDog was not my father. Which makes his clone only my half-brother. That makes sense.

Tom recalled the time in high school when his father had burst into Tom's bedroom, foaming at the mouth and proceeded to launch into a ten-minute verbal rampage, the ostensible trigger for which was Tom's failure to remember to take out the trash. But in content and duration, it was nothing short of a comprehensive and vicious litany of all Tom's adolescent transgressions and filial disappointments.

Tom had just come home from a date and was sitting on his bed reading—another annoyance that worked its way into his father's diatribe. Tom had quit the high school basketball team that winter and, almost overnight, turned into a voracious reader. One of his teachers had noticed him squinting at the blackboard and sent him to the school nurse, who promptly discovered that Tom needed glasses. In quick order, the sports trophies on the shelf above his bed were replaced by books, and his afternoon sports practices by long, pseudo-learned conversations with a group of new friends from the nerd crowd.

But the biggest chunk of the rant was about the movie Tom had seen that week and had mentioned that he liked. The movie was about a woman whose husband was fighting in Vietnam while she falls in love with a paralyzed returned vet. Based on Tom's recommendation, Mary and MadDog had gone to see it and had come home appalled. Or, in MadDog's case, over-the-top, eyes like coals, foaming at the mouth ballistic. Though the content of his rant was hardly coherent. *You think you're so smart! You don't know what sacrifice is! No son of mine...at least I think you're my son...*

That last bit got Tom's attention and MadDog's, too, apparently. Because all of a sudden, he ran out of steam and breath. Then, without another word, either of apology or explanation, he turned his back and marched upstairs. He never mentioned the subject again. And Tom didn't ask.

For the most part, he just put the incident out of his mind. MadDog going off like a primitive A-bomb was nothing unusual. Neither was his display of displeasure at any of his eldest son's acts or omissions. Clearly, in MadDog's eyes, Tom could do no right. The specifics didn't seem to matter, or at least Tom could detect no pattern. The only certainty was that he knew he would always be in trouble, no matter what he did or did not do. He'd given up trying to figure out why. By then, he was just marking time. In another year, he'd be off to college and on his own. He would just wait the maniac out.

Now, the hitherto inexplicable made sense. It was even understandable, though hardly justified. Poor Mary. Poor MadDog. Tom felt sorry for them both. A young girl stuck between a rock and a hard place, doing what she had to do. A young husband slowly awakening to an ugly truth and having to live with it every day, watching his wife's love child grow up different and disapproving. Given MadDog's temperament, Tom felt lucky to have survived adolescence.

But where did that leave him now? MadDog was dead. Mary was dead. Joe... the new and improved super badass Sheriff Morgan, was a violent mess. Who was Tom's family, now? And what was going to become of it now that the matriarch was gone?

Chapter Ten

Tom would have liked to have seen Bonnie and the kids that afternoon. Luke and the girls would be home from school. But since Joe might be there, too, it was probably best to leave logistics to Bonnie. They would see each other tomorrow at the funeral. Afterward, he and Joe could do whatever was necessary regarding their mother's estate. Or not. Then Tom would fly back to London. Tanner had made it clear that the clock was ticking, that it was *Tom's* project and that there would be no reprieve.

Instead of enjoying a few hours playing beloved uncle, he checked into one of the small, non-franchised motels at the edge of town. It might even have been the same one that Homeland Security had taken him to three years earlier to grill him about his connection to Susan Pearce and her alleged terrorist lover. The room felt familiar, as did the sound of eighteen-wheelers rumbling past the curtained, ground-floor window and the smell of deep-fried fat wafting from the fast-food place next door. Checking the bathroom, he noted the fiberglass tub/shower missing its curtain and the cracked sink that held neither soap nor towel. Yeah, it was probably the same place. Sweet dreams.

Rosemary Ryan's revelations deserved the kind of sustained attention he didn't have time for. But they could not be put aside completely. Collapsing into a lumpy bedside armchair, he closed his eyes and allowed his mind to go where it had to. *Who is my family – in both senses of the word: people with names and names with histories? And what will become of them now with the mater dominatrix gone?* He waited for his mind to provide an answer so that he could pick it apart in an iterative process that might lead to someplace useful. But his brain refused to play the game. He threw out names and identities: Mary, MadDog, some unnamed New York lawyer. His brain declined the prompts. He tried to picture his mother as a young woman and MadDog as a new husband and father. Both would have been nearly twenty younger than he was now. What could they have known? What would you have done in their place, smart boy?

His mind threw out questions like Zen koans for which there were no easy or obvious answers. But his brain remained shut. Finally, an Old Testament verse popped into his head, most likely in admonition rather than response."And the sins of the fathers shall be visited upon the children, and upon the children's children, until the third and fourth generation."

No shit.

Then his cell phone rang, yanking him back from the land of no time to the troubles of here and now. There was an ill-disguised nerviness in the voice on the other end of the line. And it took Tom a moment to pull his mind away from Coldwater and back to Europe, from problems he could not solve to ones that he could and had to.

"*La Sûreté* claim that they do not listen to *salles de conversation*," Varné began.

Tom shook his head to clear it. *Bullshit.*

"They also advise that a commercial service not try to do such in France."

Monitoring and recording conversations with the knowledge and permission of the participants was lawful everywhere in the European Union. Varné had been fed shit and shown the door. He was surprised that the Frenchman needed reassurance and direction. What had happened to the creative and enthusiastic *entrepreneur internet*?

"What prospects do you have outside of France?" Tom asked.

"One only. In Israel."

"Okay. Forget *la Sûreté* for now. When can you set up a meeting with the Israelis?"

"*La Sûreté* will make trouble..."

There was a brittleness in Varné's voice that had not been there in their prior conversations. Tom's initial impression of the Frenchman had been that he was a variation on a familiar theme: a high-energy hustler whose only real assets were charm, brains, and juice. Someone on the lookout for a promising anything he might ride until he established his own something. Surely, Varné was not the type to be discouraged by a bureaucratic fib? He tried to give the Frenchman something to reassure and, he hoped, to re-energize. "We can talk to *la Sûreté* again when the Exchange has a product. Right now, all we have is an idea."

"They will make trouble, I tell you."

"Of course they will. That's their job."

* * *

Our Lady of The Lake Catholic church had been built in the Carpenter Gothic style popular at the end of the last century. Since then, the structure had changed little, retaining its original pointed-arch, stained glass windows, board and batten siding, and steep bell tower gable. Though inside, a post-Vatican II, cloth-covered alter now faced the original rows of hardwood pews. But when the lake-facing doors remained open during summer services, the view from the sacristy remained a timeless waterscape of dappled sunlight, puffy clouds, and chill, blue water.

Tom saw that the church was sparsely filled that morning, mostly with Mary Morgan's friends from the Coldwater Senior Center. Paulie Grogan, attired in full state trooper regalia, stood at the back of the church just inside the narthex. Joe and Bonnie sat stiffly in the front pew, separated by their children. Bonnie looked straight ahead. Joe turned from time to time to survey the crowd. When he did, his eyes returned to a nearly empty pew in the back of the church where a dark-haired woman in a bright, floral, low-cut dress met his gaze and smiled. *Oh, hell, brother, why don't you just put an announcement in the Coldwater Gazette?* Across the aisle, a tall man with thinning brown hair, dressed in a nondescript blue blazer and tan trousers, seemed equally fixated on the other adult occupant of the front pew. When Joe finally noticed, he frowned for a second before returning his attention to the woman in the bright, low-cut dress. The man staring at Bonnie didn't appear to notice Joe at all.

Tom had not spoken with his brother or sister-in-law since arriving in Coldwater twenty-four hours earlier. He was not sure whether he should stand at the church door and catch them on the way out, or just show up at Joe's office the next morning. There had to be estate matters that required their attention. Tom preferred to get them out of the way as soon as possible. He did not want to appear anxious to get out of town. But he had to leave. The calls from Tanner and Varné had made that clear.

Once it began, the service was brief to the point of perfunctory. Father Gauss gave a short, generic homily on motherhood. No one else spoke. It was over in thirty minutes.

While Bonnie led the kids out of the church, Joe lagged behind to exchange words with the dark-haired lady in the floral dress. He caught up with his family while Bonnie was talking to the man in the blue blazer. "Let's go," he ordered. Bonnie ignored him. She continued to chat in a friendly voice to the man whose eyes flitted uncomfortably between her and Joe. "Who are you? Joe growled.

The man didn't answer. He seemed tongue-tied. Bonnie looked at him and spoke. "Mark, this is my husband, Joe."

The man held out a hesitant hand. Joe looked at it.

"Mark and I were in high school together."

Joe's eyes scanned him up and down.

"Let's go."

"In a minute," said Bonnie.

"Now." Joe reached for her arm.

In what Tom assumed was an instinctive, knee-jerk, gentlemanly reaction, the man in the blue blazer shot out a hand as if to intercept Joe's. It never arrived. Releasing Bonnie's wrist, Joe backhanded the man across the face. Then, in his second mistake in as many seconds, the man raised his hands as if to deliver or ward off another blow. Joe's right fist caught him flush in the pocket of bone bounded by nose, cheek, and left eye orbital. The man went down as if poleaxed, blood gushing from his nose, eye, and mouth. Bonnie grabbed the kids and ran toward the car. Paulie Grogan stepped from the narthex and placed himself between Joe and the prostrate mourner. "You'd better come with me," he said.

"What!"

"Don't make me call for backup."

Joe glared at Grogan and at the man lying on the ground.

"Get in the car," Grogan repeated. "I won't say it again."

Joe looked up and caught Tom's eye. Bonnie and the kids watched from behind rolled-up glass. Paulie Grogan herded Joe toward a dark blue state trooper sedan and drove away.

* * *

The Morgan residence consisted of a five thousand square foot, two-story log structure on ten acres of cleared land on a hillside overlooking Coldwater Lake. Surrounded on all sides by state forest, the massive structure had always struck Tom as more of a baronial lodge than a family home. The property had no neighbors, few visitors, and a security system designed to intimidate the uninvited. Two hundred decibels of PTSD-inducing siren and two thousand lumens of white halogen light would greet Tom if no one was there and he failed to punch in the current security code. His choices then would be to leave and come back later, or just leave. He'd already decided to return to London in the morning. For form's sake, if nothing else, he needed to visit with Bonnie and the kids and to make arrangements for wrapping up any estate matters with Joe, once he got out on bail for whatever the hell it was that happened at church. Other than that, Tom could think of nothing that he might accomplish by remaining in town any longer, or anything that could induce him to stay.

Had the film futures project not been on the slippery slope toward life support, he would have liked to have taken a day or two to do some sleuthing in the New York City legal directories of forty years ago. Naturally, he was curious to discover who his biological father might have been, and maybe invite the old guy to dinner if he was still around. Maybe they might have something in common other than shared DNA. But Varné's phone call was a timely reminder that Tom's career and financial survival depended on the success of a complex project that required his immediate and complete attention. If he didn't get back to Europe, the fragile project would collapse. He could not afford to let that happen.

He parked the rental car next to a post and pillar shed opposite the cabin where the only other vehicle was an ancient blue Mercury Mountaineer, dented in a dozen places and rusted through at the wheel and door panels. The car looked unlikely to pass its next emissions inspection unless some local garage owed the Coldwater sheriff a favor. Tom thought of Joe's late model, top-of-the-line, monster Silverado, which had to have cost nearly a year's pay new even before he tricked it out. *Your wife's car is a piece of shit, brother, and so are you.*

He knocked at the kitchen door, and Kate, age thirteen and already two inches taller than her mother, answered. "Uncle Tom!" Her sister Meghan appeared beside Kate and gave Tom a hard, silent hug. As dark as her sister was fair, Meghan had her father's big-boned frame and her mother's pale blue eyes. "Mom, Uncle Tom's here!" The sisters led Tom into the house, where Luke looked up from a game of chess that he was playing against himself. The boy jumped up to greet his uncle with a long, hard, silent hug like his sister's.

Bonnie came in from the back porch, holding a tall glass of something that looked like water but probably wasn't. "Ah, the elusive Tom Morgan!" The kids had changed from their funeral clothes. Their mother wore a pair of torn jeans and a loose sweatshirt.

"Hello, Bonnie."

They looked at each other awkwardly. "Kids, why don't you go down to the pond? Uncle Tom and I need to talk."

"It's too hot," said Kate.

"And buggy," said Meghan.

Luke, his arm wrapped around Tom's mid-section, said nothing. "I guess we can sit on the porch," Bonnie offered.

Tom rubbed the top of Luke's head. "Gotta talk to your mom, buddy." Luke loosened his grip, but his eyes followed Tom and his mother outside.

Bonnie seated herself in one of the Adirondack chairs facing the pond at the bottom of the property. Tom took the other chair and angled it toward her. They sat in silence until Bonnie broke it.

"I won't put up with it anymore," she said, speaking grimly to the landscape. "I can't."

Tom rubbed his jaw and suppressed the observation that he felt the same way. "If I might ask...? Who was that guy you were talking to outside the church?"

"The well-wisher who my husband put in the hospital?"

"He was staring at you the whole service, Bonnie. Joe noticed it. I noticed it. Anyone who looked at him would have."

"And my husband was looking where?"

Tom let out a short breath. "I'm not looking to cast stones, Bonnie. I'm just trying to get the lay of the land. What's happened since I left? And if it's relevant, who's doing what, with or to whom?"

Bonnie grimaced at Tom's blunt explanation and took a long swill of her drink. "Speaking for myself, nothing and nobody. As for Joe, I'd say anything with panties and a pulse. The mother of one of Kate's classmates was kind enough to share that little tidbit with me last week."

Tom lifted a hand. "I'm sorry. What can I do that won't make things worse?"

Bonne stared straight ahead. "You can make your brother disappear and then stick around to help raise his kids."

Tom looked across the sloping lawn toward the distant lake. *This could be Paradise, brother, and you're halfway to losing it. Or is your idea of Paradise being some super badass loner?*

"Tell me about this guy who Joe sucker punched," said Tom, rubbing his own jaw. "I feel like we have something in common."

Bonnie's voice was weary. "His name is Mark. We were in high school together."

"And?"

"And nothing."

Tom scoffed. "The guy looked at no one except you during the entire funeral service. Is he some kind of long-lost admirer? Someone you might be interested in?"

Bonnie smirked. "How would I find out? You saw what Joe did to the man, simply because he had the courtesy to express his condolences."

It felt like more than that.

"So, what are your plans?" he asked.

"What?"

"For when my brother gets home. Are you going to lock him out? Or are you planning to just be here and *que sera sera*?"

Bonnie looked confused and tired. "I don't know. I'm sure if I asked, Mark..." Her voice and words drifted. Then they became hard. "No. That wouldn't be fair. Or safe. You saw what Joe did to the man. Even if I might be interested, I'm not going to sell myself, or trade my children's futures, just for a safe place to stay."

Luke appeared in the doorway holding a pair of fishing rods. Tom turned his attention to his nephew and smiled. "Getting in much fishing, lately?"

Luke shook his head and answered in a Morgan family variation of Pig Latin that Tom had taught him years ago on the misrepresentation that it was a secret language passed from the eldest male Morgan in each generation to the eldest in the next. "N-**adic**-o," he said.

Bonnie looked up, seemingly startled.

"Have you got a passport, buddy?" Tom asked. Luke shrugged. Tom turned to his sister-in-law. "Do you and the kids have current passports?"

"They don't need a passport to go back and forth between here and my parents'. Not yet, anyway. Why?"

"Because I live in London, and I have to get back. But if push comes to shove, a year abroad..."

"Oh, Tom. Joe would just follow us."

"But his badge is no good there. He may be able to get away with doing what he wants in Coldwater. But not across the ocean in another country."

"He'll try."

"Then he'll find just how far his power doesn't reach. If he shows up in

London and doesn't behave himself, he'll be sharing a small, crowded cell with a bunch of skinheads."

"I don't know, Tom."

"Or Paris. You speak the language. Joe never bothered. The kids should have the chance..."

Bonnie shook her head. "That's very generous, Tom. But Coldwater is my home. I don't want to leave it." She scowled. "I want Joe to."

What Tom had to say next needed to be said. But it was unlikely to be well-received. "Then you need to find your *Beast,* Bonnie. And it's not this Mark guy."

"My what?"

A sarcastic inner voice warned Tom that the analogy he was about to share was politically incorrect, gender insensitive and undoubtedly unwelcome. But it was true. And it needed to be said. The only way Joe was going to leave Coldwater was on his shield.

"Do you remember the Disney movie *Beauty and The Beast*?" he asked.

"Vaguely."

"And what it's about?"

"Some princess who falls for an ugly monster? Why?"

"Because there's a lesson in it that you might want to think about while you're deciding what to do next about my brother."

Bonnie shifted in her seat. Tom plunged ahead.

"The woman in that movie wasn't a princess. Just an ordinary woman who attracted the attention of a bully. Then she met the Beast. She didn't want to get involved with the bully, the Beast, or anyone else. She just wanted to be left alone. But the bully wouldn't leave her alone. Fortunately, the Beast turned out to be a nice guy and she eventually warmed up to him. He was also a bigger badass than the bully, and he took care of her problem."

"Tom! I can't believe you. That's completely sexist!"

"Only if you think what I'm saying is that a woman in trouble needs a male protector. I'm not. That's not the story or the lesson. The story is about a person who finds herself in a dangerous situation that she can't escape and can't handle alone. The lesson is about the necessity of finding an ally or allies who can help in that kind of situation, and to find them before it's too late. More importantly, it's about being open to looking for help in places you might not normally think of."

"What are you trying to say, Tom?"

"That your bully just beat up your wanabe Beast, and you need a Plan B."

Chapter Eleven

Tom's cell phone buzzed as he was pulling out of Bonnie's driveway. The display warned that it was Joe. Tom had assumed there would be issues with their mother's estate. MadDog had made no preparations for his possible demise, and his widow might have been equally uncaring. But, given the events of that morning, Joe might also be calling for legal assistance or even bail. Both were unlikely. But there was no point in refusing the call.

"Get your ass down to Volz Collision."

While the call was not entirely unexpected, the fact that Joe was not in jail was. The proposed venue did not seem a likely place to sort estate issues.

"Hello, brother. I thought Paulie Grogan finally had you behind bars."

"Get your ass down here. There's something you need to see."

"Like what?" There was no point in declining to meet either, however mysterious the location. But Joe's preemptive tone irritated.

"Just get down here."

As Tom drove down Route 6 toward the commercial/industrial section of town, he tried to dismiss his irritation by recalling his and Joe's youthful encounters with Volz Collision and its owner, Hans Voltz. A German internee during WWII, Voltz and his fellow p.o.w.'s had been sent to work on the dairy farms around Coldwater, and a few had decided to stay on after VE day. Voltz eventually managed to save enough money to open an auto repair shop where he specialized in repairing European cars. Originally from the Tyrol and an avid hiker, Voltz shared his passion with his adopted community by becoming a Boy Scout leader. Tom and Joe got to know the friendly outdoorsman on numerous supervised hiking and camping trips. Then they got to know the hard-nosed, no-nonsense businessman when Voltz caught them accessorizing their Schwinn three-speed bicycles with aluminum tire caps they pilfered from a wrecked Packard in the back lot of his service garage. Tom had not been back to the scene of their boyhood mischief since then.

The shop was closed. But Tom found Joe in the lot behind it, pacing among the wrecks, junkers, and parts cars. Joe made a peremptory gesture toward the wreck of a black Silverado whose crumpled wheels were the size of tractor tires. "Look that over and tell me what jumps out at you." There was no "Hi, how've you been? How're the new front teeth working out?"

Good to see you, too, brother. Put anyone in the hospital lately?

Joe waited, arms crossed, mouth tight.

"Is this your truck?" Tom asked.

"What's left of it."

"The one Herbert Ball was driving with Mom riding shotgun?"

"That's right."

"Well, first, do you want to tell me how they got in? Those tires put the cab at least three feet off the ground. Mom couldn't have managed that on her best day."

"She got in. They both did. The story is that the boyfriend was driving, had a heart attack, and ran off the road. You tell me if what you see matches that story."

Tom walked around the crumpled metal wreck, noting the smashed roof, broken windshield, bloody upholstery, and caved-in grill and tailgate. Then he examined the tires for punctures and what was visible of the brake line for signs of tampering.

"I don't see anything consistent, or inconsistent," he said when he was done. "But then wrecked trucks aren't my specialty. What am I missing?"

Joe lifted the smashed tailgate with the toe of his boot. "This," he said, pointing to multiple streaks of pale blue paint across the truck's tailgate and on the bumper below it. "Stevie Wonder couldn't have missed that. But Paulie Grogan did, if he even looked."

"A hit and run? From behind?"

"Not one hit. This vehicle was rammed from behind at least half a dozen times."

Tom nodded and tried to process the implications. "What was Herbert doing driving your truck?"

"He was driving it, that's all. Mom was with him in the front seat. Those paint marks and dents say that they got run off the road. The question is: by who?"

"If they thought it was you, it could be anybody."

"Quit being a wise guy. Paulie Grogan is either brain-dead or looking the other way. But someone ran our mother and her boyfriend off the road and killed them. This wasn't an accident."

To Tom's surprise, he felt neither anger nor curiosity. What he felt, was irritation. *You haven't got time for this.*

Joe pressed. "So, what are you going to do?"

Tom stared at him. "What am ***I*** going to do?"

"Yes, you. Paulie Grogan isn't going to lift a finger. I'm stitched up and brain-fogged on painkillers. That leaves you."

Tom shook his head, more annoyed than confused. "Are you asking for my help?"

"I'm telling you that someone killed our mother, and I'm asking what you're going to do about it."

Tom's response was curt and visceral. "And do I lose the rest of my teeth, if the evidence leads to someplace you don't like?"

"You didn't have any evidence."

"Because you stopped me from looking."

Joe took a step closer. "This isn't MadDog. This is our mother."

"And I repeat, what happens if you don't like what I find? Do I end up taking my meals through a straw?"

"Is that a *Yes* or a *No*?"

"It's an emphatic, No."

"Then get the hell out of here. Go back to counting your shekels."

Bravado aside, Joe had nerve. The last time they had worked together,

Joe had been at pains to remind Tom that he was a lawyer, not a cop. What had changed? How was he, Tom, supposed to figure out who might have rammed into the back of Joe's truck, killing Mary and her boy toy? Where would he begin? With what resources? MadDog had been dead nearly fifteen years, and neither Joe, the state troopers, nor any of the other law enforcement agencies that had investigated the former Coldwater sheriff's murder had come anywhere near to figuring out what had happened. What was Tom Morgan, international mergers and acquisitions lawyer, supposed to accomplish by sticking around for a few days? Analyze paint samples? He didn't have time. Either he returned to Europe tonight, or a time-sensitive, career-defining project would fail spectacularly, leaving him broke.

* * *

Tom's plane to London didn't take off until 8:45 PM, which left him several hours to kill. He had promised Fr. Gauss that he'd try to stop by the rectory before he left. But when he phoned, the housekeeper told him that the priest had gone into the city for the day. He thought about stopping by his mother's condo and having one last look around. Joe was welcome to the knickknacks and memorabilia. But Tom had unanswered questions. Maybe there were clues in how and where she lived her last days.

When he pulled into the empty parking space in front of her condo, he was surprised to see the front door ajar. *Joe couldn't have emptied the place out already*? Mounting the front steps two at a time, he pushed the door open and stood staring into a room littered with overturned furniture, smashed pictures, and dents in the painted drywall as if someone had taken a baseball bat to it. From what he could remember, there was nothing obviously missing, and no pulled-out drawers or ripped cushions that might indicate someone had been looking for something. It looked more like a punk rock band had thrown a bacchanalian party and someone had decided it would be fun to trash everything not nailed down.

Beyond the bedrooms off the central hall leading to the kitchen, nothing seemed to have been disturbed. He dialed his brother's number from the wall phone in the kitchen, rather than use his cell phone which might have gone unanswered. "You'd better get over to Mom's apartment," he said, as soon as Joe picked up. "Someone's trashed it."

"What? How?"

"Like the Hellers just had a 'getting out of jail' party in the living room."

Tom listened to silence on the other end of the line, and then, "So you're staying?"

"Just get over here."

* * *

Joe walked through the apartment, closing drawers and righting furniture. Tom followed and watched. When he finished, Joe sat on the edge of their mother's couch and stared up at the ceiling. "So, what do you think?"

Tom scanned the room. "Somebody had a tantrum. But it doesn't look like they were searching for anything. The bedrooms and kitchen weren't tossed. Or whoever trashed this room found what they were looking for and didn't bother with the rest of the place."

Joe nodded.

"But I haven't been here recently enough to know if anything's missing."

Joe nodded again.

"Well, is there anything missing?"

Joe gestured at a smashed end table at the far end of the couch. "A pair of eyeglasses were on that table when I was here two days ago."

"Mom didn't wear glasses. She needed them, but she was too vain."

"The boyfriend's, then."

Tom raised his hands as if to say, "And that tells you what?"

Joe stood. "Come on. We'll check his apartment." He pulled a ring of keys from his pocket. One had a Buick symbol, and the other two looked like door and mailbox keys.

"Where'd you get those?"

"Borrowed them."

* * *

Herbert Ball's apartment was on the opposite side of the Coldwater Senior Housing Complex, across the macadam parking lot. Tom's first impression when they entered the flat was that the place was as neat and orderly as the man himself. The paintings were straight, the drawers organized and the clothes in the master bedroom closet clean and pressed. Nothing had been disturbed or seemed out of place. Even the utensils in the kitchen drawer were stacked neatly and faced the same direction. Joe opened cabinets and drawers and checked inside the stove and refrigerator. Then he pulled a plastic garbage pail from under the counter and dumped its contents into the kitchen sink. After separating some of the larger pieces, he called to Tom. "Check this."

Joe lifted what appeared to be a broken picture frame covered with food bits and torn pieces of the photograph it had once contained. He wiped the food off the photo fragments and laid them on a clean stretch of counter. Then, he started to put them together like a jigsaw puzzle.

Tom looked over his shoulder. "Someone went to town on that." The faces in the photo had been scratched out with a pen, or something like it. But the figures were clearly those of a man and a woman.

"That's him and Mom," said Joe. "That blazer is back there in his closet. And that's Mom's favorite dress."

Tom stared at the torn and food-stained photo. "What does it mean?"

"Don't know. Maybe he and Mom had a fight."

"They were off joyriding together in your truck, Joe."

"Okay. Maybe not."

"And maybe whoever was mad enough to scratch out both faces ran them off the road?"

Joe pursed his lips. "Maybe." He put the smashed picture frame and defaced photo into a plastic baggie that he took from a drawer beside the sink. "See if you can find a pair of wire-framed eyeglasses somewhere."

The night table next to the bed in the master bedroom seemed like a likely place to find a pair of spectacles. Though, if they were Herbert's,

Tom wasn't clear why their presence or absence should mean anything. Opening the bedside drawer, he was surprised to see an untidy jumble of pens, highlighters, bookmarks, and crumpled notepaper, very unlike the neatly organized storage places in the rest of the apartment.

Joe came into the room and looked into the open drawer. "Find anything?"

"No glasses. But someone's been through here and didn't leave things the way they found them." He gestured at the open drawer. "Herbert Ball wouldn't shove stuff in a drawer like that. The guy was a neat freak." From beneath the clutter, Tom retrieved a gold ring with a red stone center, wheat chaff sides and a raised numeral '47' over the words 'Cornell University Law School'. " Did Mom ever mention that her boyfriend went to law school?"

"No. And neither did he." Joe took the ring and squinted at the faded letters inscribed inside the band. "HB…? Then something after that, but it's rubbed off." He handed it back to Tom. "Maybe he was a junior or something."

Tom examined the faded inscription. "Guys like Herbert Ball aren't juniors. They're the thirds, fourths, and fifths." He dropped the ring back in the drawer.

Joe ran the side of a pencil across the notepad lying on the night table. "Well, you're right. Someone's been through here. Probably in a hurry." Tom returned to the living room and began to open drawers that Joe had already gone through. Joe watched from the hallway. "What are you doing?"

Tom looked around the apartment, closed the drawer and turned to face his brother. "I don't know. That's the problem."

Joe said nothing.

"I don't know what I'm doing, and I haven't got time to figure it out. Mom's apartment has been tossed, and this place has been searched. Someone drove her and her boyfriend off the road. Whether they intended to kill them or even knew it was them, who knows? You're stitched up like a piece of cheap luggage and popping painkillers like juju beans. But if I don't get back to my job by yesterday, I'm going to end up broke. There's nothing I can do here to be helpful in the time I've got, which is basically no time."

"Someone killed our mother, Tommy."

"Oh, and your wife's going to leave you."

"That's none of your business."

"None of this is my business, Joe. I'm not a cop. And if I'm reading the neon right, you're not going to be one much longer."

"What are you saying?"

"I'm saying that Paulie Grogan wants your job, someone with a bow and arrow wants you dead, your wife wants out, and your police skills are down to maim it or kill it. I can't help you with any of that."

"Then just help me find out who killed our mother."

Tom took a deep breath. Why did he feel torn? What were the chances of accomplishing anything in the next few days compared to the consequences of remaining? And why, knowing that, did he still hear himself say, "I can give you two days."

Joe scoffed. "Then you'd better work fast."

Chapter Twelve

Tom checked back into his motel room and tried to think through what he could and needed to do next. Tanner Hartwell should have gotten back to him by now. Yvette Huppe was probably chewing her arm off at his continued silence. After brewing a weak cup of coffee in the room's one-cup Mr. Coffee machine, he decided to call Tanner first. The conversation got off to a bad start and went downhill from there.

"The client won't put in any money," said Tanner. "But the chairman says that he was contacted by a UK bank that expressed interest in participating in the project. He's going to meet with their representatives this week."

Tom suppressed a surge of exasperation. Tanner had to know that any expression of interest by a UK bank had to be bogus. If the bankers came at all, it would be to kill a potential competitor, not fund one. He tried to keep the emotion from his voice. "You told him that no UK bank is actually going to cut a check, right? That it will hire McKinsey to study the project and put it on permanent hold."

Tanner's voice managed to sound bland and hard at the same time. "The chairman thinks the bank might be willing to provide funds for a three-year supply contract. If so, his accountants will allow the company to book revenue this quarter. That would solve his company's problem without the need for further investment."

Tom was incredulous. A sophisticated deal lawyer like Hartwell could not possibly credit either the UK bank story or the sleight of hand accounting. With an effort to keep his voice short of a shout, Tom listed the obvious problems. "Unless this bank has the time, talent, and incentive to do something by January 1st that nobody has ever done before, our firm's biggest client is going to have to reverse any revenue it books, almost immediately. Then the analysts will eviscerate management, the outside directors will force them to resign, and our firm will look incompetent or worse for letting them do something so stupid. Our firm's biggest client is heading for a train wreck, Tanner. You've got to talk them out of it."

Tom listened for the familiar scratch of pen on paper, but there was only silence. When Hartwell spoke, he sounded tired, and what came from his mouth sounded rehearsed. Tom wasn't sure which was more ominous.

"I told management the same thing, Tom, albeit less dramatically. Nevertheless, without the company's further investment or outside financing, your project won't launch in time to meet their needs. And our partners' committee has never been comfortable with the firm having a quasi-equity interest in a speculative investment. They only agreed because you convinced them it would help an important client in a difficult situation. Since that now appears unlikely, the firm will have to reevaluate its involvement and resume normal billing at the very least ."

Deference may have been called for. But Tom could not keep the curtness from his voice. "And if I can secure financing from an outside source that actually wants to see the project succeed? Will the firm hold off billing until the exchange is launched?"

"The free ride is over on January 1st, Tom."

It didn't take long for Tom to review his options. He didn't have any. If both the firm and the client discontinued their financial support, the project was dead. Something like a film futures exchange was still needed. If the European film industry could manage to limp along for a few more years, someone would eventually show up and do it. But that someone would not be Tom Morgan. By then, he'd be broke, his once vibrant career the fatal casualty of a self-inflicted wound.

Not so smart now, are we, bright boy?

He decided to put off making the phone call to Yvette Huppe. What was he going to say? Got a spare hundred million euros? He needed time to think and to think of one thing at a time. Though all his brain served up was Joe's smarmy challenge to "work fast."

Think of something, Tommy. Dithering is not a strategy.

Leaving the motel, he climbed into the rental car and headed once more down the lake road toward Our Lady of The Lake church. Yvette Huppe could wait.

Mrs. Flynn led him down the uncarpeted hall to Father Gauss's study. The priest sat where Tom had left him, in a cracked leather chair behind an old wood trestle table, scribbling something onto a lined notepad. "Ah, Thomas," said Gauss, looking up from his work. "Thanks for stopping by before you skipped town. I don't get to see enough of you these days. Never, it seems, under happy circumstances. Sit down."

Tom took the chair opposite and began with a blunt, "My mother was murdered."

Gauss's eyes widened.

"Joe found evidence that the truck she was killed in was rammed from behind multiple times before it went off the road and crashed."

"Dear God."

"I've just come from her apartment which has also been trashed. Her boyfriend's place has been searched, too."

Gauss folded his hands and said a silent prayer. When he looked up, he asked, "Do you have to go back to Europe right away?"

"I should. My business there is falling apart as we speak. But my brother claims that he and I can figure out 'who done it' in a few days if we put our heads together."

"Is that likely?"

"No."

Gauss lifted his hands. "How can I help?"

"If you would, listen to me riff for a few minutes. Then, if you have any advice, I'd be grateful to hear it."

Gauss settled back into his chair.

"I don't know what my brother intends to do. We're still circling each other like rival dogs. But if the truck my mother was killed in was deliberately run off the road, then whoever did it either thought Joe was driving, or they were after Herbert Ball and/or my mother. If they were after Joe, then he's in the best position to come up with suspects. But if the killer was after Ball or my mother, then my asking some basic questions and running obvious leads might lead to answers. Otherwise, I don't see what I can do here in just a few days. If it turns out nothing, I'll go back to making a living while the option is still open."

Gauss asked. "Are any of these basic questions ones I might help with?"

"One." Tom felt awkward, knowing what he was about to ask. But there was no alternative. If he didn't ask, there was no reason for his being here, and he had nowhere else to go. "People tell you things," he said. "And you hear things. Who's doing what with who, and who does or doesn't know about it? Who's mad at who and why? Who's got a grudge that goes back into the mists of time."

"I'm afraid..."

"I don't mean for you to violate a confidence, Father. But my mother was a parishioner at Our Lady of The Lake for practically forever. Was there anything she might have done to inspire murder? Anything that you can tell me?"

"Oh, Tommy..."

"Or maybe not murder. Maybe just something sufficient to inspire a bumper a tap at an opportune moment."

Gauss took a deep breath. "Your mother was a difficult woman, Tommy. But I'm not aware of any transgressions that might have inspired murder. As for something that might inspire a spontaneous bumper tap? Who among us hasn't?"

Tom slumped in his chair. "I'm grasping at air, aren't I?"

"I'm sorry. But at the risk of opening old wounds, have you spoken with your mother's friend, Rosemary Ryan?"

"Not about this. I could, if she hasn't already left town, and if she'll talk to me."

"Yes. You and she have a bit of history."

More than you know.

Tom continued, reshuffling suspects and victims. "How about Herbert

Ball, the driver? Can you think of a reason why someone might have wanted to give him a gentle nudge off the planet?"

Gauss pressed his fingers together under his chin. "Mr. Ball wasn't a parishioner of our church. In fact, I never met him. But his name had a habit of coming up from time to time. It seems he had a reputation as a ladies' man, if that helps."

"Enough of a ladies' man for someone to want to kill him?"

"That seems unlikely."

"Or run him off the road?"

Gauss shrugged. "'Hell hath no fury…,' or, so I'm told."

* * *

After consuming a few more pastries, Tom left the rectory and drove toward Wilson Point. His attention now turned toward how best to approach Mrs. Ryan one more time. What exactly was he going to ask? *Got any more dirt on my mother? Like, what she might have done to inspire someone to kill her?* Rosemary Ryan wasn't going to want to see her former pupil again so soon, or perhaps ever. He wasn't sure that he wanted to see her again. But there was no one else likely to have answers to the questions that needed to be asked.

Tom eased his rental car down the nearly vertical slope and found Andrew Ryan standing in his driveway raking leaves. A dark blue Mercedes that had belonged to Ryan's deceased wife sat parked beside the house, covered in twigs and wet leaves. "If you're looking for mother," said Ryan, "you just missed her."

"Do you know when she might be back?"

"In the spring, I imagine. She's gone back to Florida for the winter."

Tom looked past Ryan at a blanket of whitecaps frothing the lake. Winter would be here soon. "That's too bad. I really need to speak to her."

"Is there anything I can help with?"

"I don't think so. More questions about my mother. Mrs. Ryan was very helpful when I was here last."

"Do you have her number?" Tom shook his head. "Let me get it for you."

Ryan went inside the house. While Tom waited, a sudden breeze scattered the pile of leaves that Ryan had been raking, blowing a patch in the wet debris that covered the front of the parked Mercedes. A dented and misaligned hood appeared where the wet debris had been.

When Andrew reappeared, he held a piece of green notepaper in an outstretched hand. "This is an old recipe mother wrote down for me with her number at the bottom. I'm supposed to call her if I run into culinary difficulty. She thinks I should learn to cook. I don't. Please feel free to keep it."

"Thanks," said Tom, taking the paper and then gesturing at the dented Mercedes. "The notorious Ryan driveway claims another victim?"

Andrew grimaced. "Mother shouldn't drive anymore. But try telling her that. Thankfully, no one was hurt."

Tom opened the car door. "You know, there might be something you can help me with. I was going to ask your mother about Herbert Ball, the guy who was driving the truck that ran off the road and killed him and my mom. So far, the Coldwater Hospital and the sheriff's department haven't been able to locate his next of kin. If he were a depositor at your bank, would you have the name and address of a beneficiary?"

Ryan looked uncomfortable. "I can confirm that he was a depositor. One of our largest, in fact. And I could let you know if we have a beneficiary of record. But I'll need a written request from the sheriff's office to release it."

"That's fine. I'll let my brother know." Tom folded the note paper and put it in his pocket. "Please give Maggie my best when you talk to her."

Andrew dipped his chin. But he didn't smile.

* * *

The phone call from Yvette Huppe came through while Tom was driving toward town. He pulled off to the side of the road to take it.

"You blew *le Weekend,*" she began. "Do you realize that? *Complètement.*"

Perhaps it was a bad transatlantic connection, but Huppe's voice came through like a shout in a wind tunnel. Tom felt the muscles of his face tighten. "I gave my pitch; the distributors and exhibitors gave theirs. On a project like this, you either start with a common vision, or every unanticipated problem becomes an excuse to exit. We can't afford that."

"A vision, yes. But you must build, too, and quickly. Did you leave with new friends? New ideas?"

"A Monsieur Varné pitched an interesting idea for collecting data from internet chat rooms. That's not in our business plan, but it could be an interesting option down the road."

"I do not mean ideas without money. The distributors have box office data. You and Monsieur Varné have neither data nor money. Worse, you are not of *le club*. The distributors may have needed your idea and a kick in the pants. But now they've had both, they may think they no longer need *you*."

Tom scoffed. "If a bunch of film distributors try to launch a new kind of financial clearinghouse, they'll lose both their money *and* their independence. If they have that kind of risk capital, they'd be smart to give it to me. I won't lose it."

"Then you must get back here now, or they will try." There was a pause on the other end of the line. "I will come to London tomorrow. There is much to discuss."

"I'm not in London, Yvette. I'm in the States, and I have to remain here for a few more days."

After a moment of cell phone static, her voice came through clearly, "That is risky, Tom. I cannot promise what you will find if you don't return now."

"I'll be back the day after tomorrow."

* * *

As soon as he returned to his motel, Tom's phone buzzed again. The voice on the other end was a surprise, though perhaps it should not have been. Simon Woodson had been a law school classmate who married a UK barrister and now managed the London office of a small mergers and acquisitions firm. Other than occasionally bumping into each other at the Cornell Club in New

York, Tom had not seen or spoken to Woodson in nearly a decade. "Simon! To what do I owe?"

"I'm calling to save your European film futures project."

"My what?

Woodson laughed. "The whole town knows what you're up to, Morgan."

Crap.

"Look, I'll cut to the chase. My client is the Midlands Farmers' Cooperative. Their managing director called me today. Barclays has been to see him about taking an equity interest in their pig operations."

Tom felt his stomach clench. "Let me guess: separately incorporated with a pan-European charter of operations?"

"Bingo. Which is what made me think of you. I remembered that wacky discussion we had back in law school where you thought flexible charter companies might be used to avoid EU regulation. I thought you were crazy then. But from what I'm hearing ... well, this European film futures thing has Tom Morgan written all over it."

"What are they offering?"

"A hundred million euros."

"Good luck collecting."

"Would you care to make a better offer? That's why I'm calling."

Tom hesitated. Was Simon fishing on behalf of his client, or their bank? After a moment's thought, he decided that it didn't matter. "I could make a more realistic offer," he said. "If that's of interest. An offer your client might actually collect on."

"I'm listening."

After a pause to gather his thoughts, Tom elaborated, "Your client's charter could be worth a premium of 10x or zero, depending on whether someone can use it to get a new kind of financial exchange up and running without regulatory approval. No UK bank is going into the film futures business. Their offer is designed to block one. Your client is not going to get a hundred million euros upfront. Or even a fraction of that. Ever. What it's going to get is endless negotiation and delay."

"That's why I called, Tom. What kind of *realistic* offer might I pass on to my client?"

Tom scribbled a note for the file while he spoke. "Reverse merger: acquisition company into pig exchange. Your client gets fifteen percent of the merged entity. When the futures exchange launches, it'll make a killing."

"And if it doesn't launch?"

"Then we dissolve the merger, and your client is back in the pig business where they started. But they haven't lost anything. And no one is wasting their time or blowing smoke up their skirts."

Chapter Thirteen

Tom left the motel early and started the long drive to his and Herbert Ball's *alma mater*. Meandering along two-lane back roads at an average speed of growing grass, he replayed his conversation with Yvette Huppe and kept an eye out for early morning deer. He wasn't worried that the European distributors might take over and complete the film exchange project. Other than box office data, the distributors lacked all the other necessary pieces, including technical expertise, deep pockets, and studio support. But Madame Huppe had seemed convinced that they might try. If they did, their efforts were sure to end in disaster, not just for them, but for Tom Morgan, as well. He had told Joe that he would give him two days. But the only sensible thing now was to get back to Europe, fast. He would find what he could in Ithaca and then drive to Syracuse to catch an evening flight to London. Joe would be pissed, but that was the least of Tom's worries now.

To avoid the distraction of second-guessing, Tom turned his attention to the scenery along the two-lane back roads and to the memories it conjured. There was no direct route through the patchwork of dairy farms and state forest that blanketed New York's Northern Tier. What might have been a two-hour drive, as the crow flies, could be as much as six, depending on the vehicle and weather. How many times had he made this trip, almost always in an ancient vehicle of the penniless student variety, with no heat, rusted floorboards, and leaking compression inadequate to the innumerable hills, even with the assistance of pedal-to-the-metal running starts?

Fall and spring along the Finger Lakes could be beautiful, even when overheating radiators and bald tires commanded constant vigilance. A drive at those times was a welcome invitation to quiet reflection. But winter drives could be a white knuckle nightmare, given the ever-present possibility of becoming stranded on the side of the road on a bitterly cold and snowy night, in the days before cell phones, with few passing cars and fewer inclined to stop for stranded motorist of youthful age, male gender, and penniless appearance.

The winding route finally straightened near the top of Lake Cayuga. The state road that hugged the western shoreline was deceptively cozy in the bright morning sunlight. Adjusting the car's electric seat heater, Tom found himself revisiting the homily that Father Gauss had given at Mary's funeral. The brief sermon had seemed little more than Cliff Notes on the Jungian archetype of Mother: loving and nurturing, a creative force not just for life but for art and ideas, as well. But no one who listened that day and who knew Mary Morgan even casually would have recognized any of it. Braver might have been a homily on the archetypal 'Terrible Mother': force of death and destruction. Though, after Rosemary Ryan's revelations, he realized that neither was true. His mother remained a mystery, even if he knew more about her now than he had a few days ago.

From Mrs. Ryan's disclosures, he felt that he had some idea now of what made his mother the way she was. But who might she have been if she hadn't run, back-to-back, into the no-escape nightmares of an unwed pregnancy and shotgun marriage to MadDog Morgan? How could anyone have discovered who they were and what they wanted to be if they were launched into adulthood as she had been? If Mary Morgan had a chance, it must have seemed an impossibly small one, with a sanguinary splat if she failed. How many people in that era and under those circumstances would have had the courage to tough it out and take the consequences? Could he blame her that she hadn't?

Lost in thought, it was nearly Noon before he arrived in Ithaca. Much had changed since he was there last. Collegetown had been cleaned up. The municipal garbage cans were no longer spilling trash onto the streets. There were fewer bars and more coffee shops. Driving slowly across the Cornell campus, he snagged a parking spot in front of the Johnson Art Museum and strolled from there to the Arts Quad. The oak trees that had been planted to replace the Dutch Elms wiped out by disease in the 1970s, had finally reached the beginnings of stately maturity. Though the current crop of undergraduates who passed beneath them looked depressingly like high school students and not nearly as well dressed. Meandering across the Quad, he ducked into a few old classrooms and remained to wallow in wistful nostalgia. He knew that he needed to get on with what he came there to do: find something useful about Herbert Ball. But he took his time before heading over to the law school, stopping at Zinks for a cup of coffee and to peruse a copy of the student newspaper, the Cornell Daily Sun. Eventually, he made his way over to the law school.

Unlike the rest of the campus, the law school did not appear to have changed much since he was there last. No doubt that was not an accident. The law school's Collegiate Gothic buildings, including the landmark law library and Moot Court, were the iconic gateway to the rest of the university campus. It would take more than an ambitious administrator and deep-pocket donor to alter or modernize that imposing exterior.

He briefly explained his purpose to a woman seated behind the chest-high oak and brass cage barrier at the Admissions Office. "One of your graduates died recently in an automobile accident near Coldwater, New York. The sheriff's department there hasn't been able to locate a next of kin. I've been asked to see if his alma mater might have any useful records. His name was Herbert Ball, class of 1947."

"I don't know. Mr...?"

"Morgan."

The woman seemed uncertain. "Do you have some identification?" He took out his wallet and handed over his international driver's license. She looked at it and then peered at him. "Thomas J. Morgan?"

"That's right."

"Are you an alumnus of the law school, as well, Mr. Morgan?"

"Nearly twenty years ago."

She nodded and smiled. "You look better in person than in your newspaper photos. Without the bandages, I mean."

Tom laughed. "And I'm trying to stay that way."

"Wait here, and I'll see what I can find."

Tom had mixed feelings about his fifteen minutes of fame. He sometimes wondered if he might have discovered who killed his former girlfriend's little brother without getting her, and nearly himself, killed as well. The news outlets had painted Tom Morgan a hero for saving half the East Coast from a biochemical attack. But the story was bogus. Dr. Hassad was no terrorist. But by the time the Coldwater Gazette printed the real story, the national print and television media had moved on to the next breathless headline. The New York Times, which had carried the phony story on its front page for nearly a week, never printed a retraction. Later, when the Gazette won a Pulitzer for "uncovering" the real story, no one outside of Coldwater paid much attention. The name Tom Morgan seemed destined to remain forever linked to that infamous "terrorist" Suliman Twafik, and the name Coldwater to a foiled biochemical attack that never was.

The friendly admissions lady returned with a faded cloth-bound ledger and a Class of 1947 Year Book. "I checked the registers for 1946 through 1949," she said. "There's no Herbert Ball listed in any of them. But I brought these in case you wanted to look for yourself."

Tom spread the register open on the polished wood counter and looked carefully through the entries for 1947. There was no listing for a Herbert Ball. But as he flipped pages in the 1947 Yearbook, a name and a photo caught his eye: Herbert B. Shea. The young man in the photo had a full head of hair, and his nose and ears were somewhat smaller. But the self-assured look of a handsome rogue was familiar. "Do you have any records on this student?"

"Did he die in an accident, too?"

"I don't know. But he's a ringer for the guy who did, minus about sixty years."

"I'll look."

When the woman disappeared into the labyrinth, Tom took a seat on the wooden bench outside the Dean of Admissions office. There, he tried without success to repress the memory of the last time he had sat on that bench. He was well aware at the time, of why he had been summoned. But he had no idea of what would happen next. A first year law student who gets into a public pissing contest with a tenured professor cannot expect a happy outcome.

His problem hadn't been so much with the professor, although he was a pompous ass. It had been more with the Socratic method as it was then used, and often misused, by certain law professors. The ancient pedagogical method typically involves asking a series of questions that can only be answered in a finite number of ways. At the end of the exercise, the responder finds that he's been led down a path to a response that, while obviously absurd, is nevertheless unavoidable given his prior responses. It's an uncomfortable position, especially if you count yourself among the best and the brightest, as most first-year Ivy League law students do. For that reason alone, certain professors took a perverse delight in using the method.

Tom and the maddeningly superior individual who taught First Year Criminal Law had clashed on several occasions. A former ACLU defense attorney, the professor enjoyed crossing swords with the son of a cop who, by upbringing and temperament, did not hold the knee-jerk belief that all criminal defendants are unquestionably innocent. But, as the professor controlled the questions and hence the exercise, he always came out on top in those verbal skirmishes. Until he didn't.

The night before the incident that brought Tom to the wooden bench outside the Dean of Admissions office, he had spent several hours drowning some now-forgotten sorrow at one of the Collegetown bars. So he wasn't feeling his feisty best when Professor Nelson called on him in class the next morning. As Tom recited the facts of the case and answered one leading question after another, the professor's tone became more haranguing and more sarcastic than usual. While the class generally enjoyed a bit of blood sport, as the professor's voice became more agitated and Tom's answers more curt, the assembly grew quiet. The former ACLU firebrand seemed to be heading toward something more that morning than simply making his favorite whipping boy look foolish.

Then it came. In a tone that was nearly a shout, the professor asked the final question in a form that could only be answered: yes, no, or I don't know. None of which were true or remotely satisfactory. When Tom gave his answer, the professor left his podium, approached the wooden table that was the only object separating him from his victim, and there proceeded to pound the table with a closed fist while bellowing at the top of his lungs, inches from Tom's face. "But what about *justice*, Mr. Morgan? What about *justice*!"

And that's how Tom found himself later that day sitting on the hard wooden bench outside the Dean of Admissions office, wondering if his law school career was over even before it had begun. He didn't regret his answer or his dismissive tone of voice. But he probably shouldn't have laughed. "With respect, Professor," he'd said, in a tone that was as calm and uninflected as his tormentor's was neither, "Criminal Law has about as much to do with justice as medicine has with immortality." The collective gasp was instantaneous, followed by a slow-building tsunami of raucous laughter. The professor's face blossomed to the shade of a ripe tomato as he lifted a trembling arm and thrust it toward the classroom door. "Get out of my classroom, Mr. Morgan!" he choked. "Get out! And don't come back!"

Later, Tom came to the more charitable view that law school, like military boot camp, can sometimes call for the use of methods, that while seemingly harsh and pointless, were nevertheless effective in preparing its recipients for the Darwinian environment they were about to enter. Though the availability of such methods might trigger the occasional latent sadist, the method itself could be beneficial.

When the Admissions woman finally returned, it was with a thin manila folder and a puzzled look. "There's not much," she said. "Transcripts, tuition payments, and so forth. But I found this." She opened the folder to a page containing a typed list of Herbert B. Shea's annual donations to the law school. The list ended abruptly in 1986 with the handwritten entry: *disbarred*.

Wow. Tom made a note on the back of the recipe that Andrew Ryan had given him, thanked the admissions woman, and took off on foot toward Uris Library, where the university housed its extensive collection of periodicals and newspaper microfiche. Maybe there would be something on Herbert Shea's disbarment there. Passing the McGraw clock tower, he looked up and recalled what was arguably the most famous prank in the university's history. In the fall of 1997, passersby noticed what appeared to be a Halloween pumpkin impaled nearly two hundred feet above the ground on the pinnacle of the clock tower. Who put it there, why and how, had yet to be discovered. It was a feat that would have challenged Spider-Man, and in the decade that had passed, it had already become legend.

Entering the library, he descended the narrow staircase to the third-level basement, where a few hours perusing old newspaper microfiche provided the information he was looking for. Herbert Ball, aka Herbert Ball Shea, had been a partner in the New York law firm of Reynolds, Rubinstein, and Shea, which had collapsed during the savings and loan crisis of the mid-1980s. Shea and his partners, it appeared, had been up to their eyeballs in a financial scam that later came to be known as "linked financing."

Tom remembered the savings and loan crisis well. He had just graduated from law school when the Coldwater Savings and Loan that held both his savings and his student debt went belly up. For him and a lot of other people for whom their local savings and loan was the go-to financial institution, the crisis was a multi-year nightmare. Tom eventually recovered ten cents on the dollar for his savings, but his student loan debt remained intact. Others suffered worse. Before the crisis was over, more than a third of the country's savings and loans had failed, and depositors and shareholders had lost more than $160 billion.

Later, it was said that anyone who could do simple arithmetic should have seen what was coming. In the fall of 1979, the Federal Reserve began to raise interest rates in an effort to stop inflation. The savings and loan associations were caught in a squeeze between the low-interest income they received from the fixed-rate mortgage loans that were their principal source of business and the suddenly and dramatically increased interest rates that they had to pay to attract deposits. That's where the firm of Reynolds, Rubinstein, and Shea got itself in trouble.

As the savings and loans chased higher and higher rates of return to offset inadequate returns from fixed-rate mortgages, a cottage industry of brokers sprang up to steer depositors to the institutions offering the highest interest rates on certificates of deposits. A small group of those brokers instituted a scam where the broker would approach a savings and loan with the promise to steer large numbers of depositors its way, provided the institution lent a portion of the money back to certain people designated by the broker. The designated borrowers were then paid to apply for the loans and to deliver the proceeds to the broker. When the dust settled on the decade-long crisis, the law firm of Reynolds, Rubinstein, and Shea was found to be the principal legal adviser to virtually all the crooked deposit brokers. Several of the firm's partners were subsequently disbarred, among them Herbert Ball Shea.

I guess I would have changed my name, too. On the drive to the Syracuse airport, Tom stopped at a roadside diner to eat and to call Joe with an update on his visit with Andrew Ryan and what he had found in the Cornell Law School and library archives.

"I don't follow the financial flim flam, Tommy," Joe complained when Tom had finished his summary. "What's it got to do with who killed our mother?"

"Everything. Or nothing. Suppose whoever rammed the back of your truck was after Herbert Ball Shea, not you. The number of people who might like to take a crack at Herbert, the con man, must be pretty long. He didn't shorten his name just because he was embarrassed."

Joe muttered something inaudible.

"You're going to want to pull Andrew Ryan's Mercedes, too, and check the paint against the marks on what's left of your truck."

"You think Rosemary Ryan was an angry savings and loan depositor?"

"I think Andrew Ryan knew Herbert Ball better than he let on. Ryan and his partners bought the assets of the Coldwater Savings and Loan from the Resolution Trust Corporation after the S&L went bust, and they used those assets to start what's now Coldwater Bank. I'd like to know where they got the financing and whether Andrew Ryan was ever in the mortgage broker business."

Joe grumbled, "Okay. I don't really follow this, Tommy. But it sounds like you need to have another chat with Andrew Ryan."

"I can't, Joe. You'll have to do it. I'm on my way to the airport."

"You said that you'd give me two days, Tommy."

"I know. But then I got a call about a deal I've put most of my savings into. It's run into problems. And if I don't get back to fix them, I'm going to lose everything I put in. Which is basically everything I have. Or had."

"Tommy..."

"Look, brother, I've given you the Shea/Ryan connection. That's either the answer to who killed Mom, or it isn't. But it's going to take more than two days to sort out, and I don't have two days."

Joe's voice sounded suddenly weak, and his response had nothing to do with his brother's financial troubles. "My gut's leaking, Tommy, and the painkillers have stopped working. I've got to check myself back into the hospital."

"I'm sorry," said Tom, voicing a contrition he didn't feel. He didn't know if Joe was telling the truth, exaggerating, or in genuine extremis. But it didn't matter. "You don't have to follow up on any of this tomorrow. Herbert Ball Shea isn't going anywhere. And neither is Andrew Ryan."

Joe continued to talk as if nothing Tom said had registered. "And that guy who was bothering Bonnie at mom's funeral got himself a lawyer."

It's about time somebody did.

"He's trying to get my bail revoked."

Good.

"At least talk to Andrew Ryan before you flake out on me. If that Wall Street gobbledygook is the key to figuring out who killed Mom, it's got to be you who follows up. I wouldn't know where to begin. You know that."

Tom stared at the phone. *Damn it.*

"Answer me, Tommy. Are you going to crap out on Mom? Now?"

Tom responded through clenched teeth. "I'll drive back to Coldwater and talk to Andrew Ryan first thing in the morning. But then I'm on a plane. After that..." He left the thought unfinished. *After that, what?*

Chapter Fourteen

Where does obligation end when work is the source of pride and fulfillment and family a quagmire of dysfunction and deceit? Tom had been asking himself variations on that question for most of his adult life. On the drive back to Coldwater, he went there again, recalling a television interview with Sugar Ray Leonard in which the champion boxer claimed that selfishness is a necessary ingredient of success. At the time, Tom had found the assertion distasteful, though many of the successful people he knew seemed to verify it. He preferred the arguments for balance, notwithstanding his own failure to achieve it. The problem, as he saw it, was that in the case of work and family, the unstated assumption was that both were positive. If one was great and the other awful, balance did not seem that desirable. Of course, that was not the truth of his own work/family dynamic. His career, while challenging and lucrative, was not what he wanted it to be. And his family, while broken and dysfunctional, was no horror show.

So?

So kick the can down the road. He had to get back to Europe. Finding out who killed his mother was important. But destroying his career to do it was foolish. Pursuing both at the same time was impossible. As for fixing his broken family…? He had no idea of how to do that. Or even if it could be done.

Back in Coldwater, he checked into the motel, made a few notes and then crashed into bed. At 3:00 am, a phone call from Karlheinz Klopp interrupted his troubled sleep.

"My lawyers don't like you," Klopp grumbled. "They say you are too clever, and much can go wrong."

Tom took a moment to get his bearings and find his voice. "That's what lawyers are paid to say," he finally answered. "They don't have your vision, Herr Klopp."

"Don't butter me, Tom."

Tom struggled to suppress the image and will himself awake. "Look, Karlheinz, I'm in the States. It's three o'clock in the morning here. I'm going to put the phone down and make a cup of coffee. Can you wait?"

"Yes, of course. I am sorry. Madame Huppe mentioned that you recently lost your mother. I should have known that you'd be in the United States."

Tom put a coffee packet into the countertop machine, and by the time it brewed, he was awake and ready to deal with the German.

"I'm back," he said, picking up the phone. "And I'm not *buttering* you, Karlheinz. If you're not interested in the financial celebrity role, then Featherstone or someone else can do it."

"*Was ist das?* What celebrity role?"

Tom hesitated. There was risk in letting a man like Karlheinz Klopp think that he was in the driver's seat. He knew what motivated the German, but he could not afford to waste time on diplomatic fan dancing. "If you want to be a player in Europe, Karlheinz, and not just in Germany, this is your ticket. Whoever becomes the face of the first and only global film futures exchange is going to be the next financial rock star. If you want it, it's yours. If not..."

"Ha! Rock star! If this thing you are making becomes truly global, perhaps, yes. But if the market sees only another American financial gimmick..."

Tom dealt the rest of his cards in rapid succession. "Your face. Front page spread in the London Financial Times, two-story billboard in Trafalgar Square. What else?"

Klopp responded without hesitation. "Fifty-one percent of profits in the Federal Republic."

Tom could picture the German's crocodile smile at the other end of the line. Klopp had obviously decided exactly what he wanted and had made up his mind before making the phone call.

"There are many hands," Klopp continued. "You need not trouble yourself with details."

Tom hesitated. 'Many hands' could have any number of meanings, and the German's unabashed guile made him uneasy. In that way, Klopp reminded Tom of Joe. Both were masters of their respective fiefdoms and not shy about exercising their prerogatives. In Coldwater, you dealt with Joe Morgan and the other powers that be. In Baden-Baden you dealt with Karlheinz Klopp. If not, you went home. Tom had dealt with more than a few parochial potentates, and he had learned how to engage them without losing his shirt or his moral compass. But when you play on their turf, and of necessity by their rules, it can be hard at times to keep sight of what separates you from them.

In the end, though, the film exchange could not operate without German box office data, and Karlheinz Klopp controlled the only comprehensive source. It was either throw the greedy dog a bone or call it quits and go home.

"Deal," he finally muttered. Then he hung up the phone and went into the bathroom to wash his hands. He did not look in the mirror.

* * *

The Coldwater Savings Bank occupied a two-story stone building next to a blacktopped parking lot on the lake shore side of Route 6. Its neighbors were a Chevron gas station and a local sporting goods shop. Tom arrived at the bank when it opened at 9:00 am, stopping at the first desk beyond the brass framed glass doors and fibbing to its occupant that he had an appointment with Mr. Ryan.

A helpful young woman led him through a waist-high brass gate to a set of carpeted stairs that led to the second floor. Andrew Ryan's office took up the back corner of the building and boasted a commanding view of the lake. When Tom appeared at his door, Ryan's face betrayed both surprise and annoyance. Removing a pair of wire-rimmed glasses, he gestured toward a small grouping of furniture near a fake fireplace.

"I'm sorry you came all this way," he said after they were both seated. "As I said on the phone, I wasn't able to locate a beneficiary for any of Mr. Ball's accounts."

Tom studied the banker. This wasn't going to be easy. *Mr. Ryan, are you a crook? Did you take Herbert Ball's tainted money to start Coldwater Bank? And did you make your personal pile by brokering phony loans to the old Coldwater Savings and Loan and others before they went under?*

"I'd like to look at a list of the bank's current shareholders," said Tom.

Ryan looked surprised. "I'm afraid that information is confidential. And I don't see how it might help identify Mr. Ball's next of kin."

"So, Mr. Ball wasn't a shareholder of the bank or any of its corporate shareholders?"

"I'm afraid..."

"How about a Mr. Herbert Ball Shea?"

The banker's face lost its color. His eyes scanned the room, avoiding Tom's.

"You used to be a mortgage broker," said Tom. "Before you and your partners bought the assets of the old Coldwater Savings and Loan. Isn't that right?"

Andrew Ryan looked like he was going to barf. "Why are you asking?"

"Because Herbert Ball didn't simply suffer a heart attack and run his vehicle off the road, killing him and my mother. There's evidence now that before it crashed, the vehicle they were riding in was hit repeatedly from behind. If whoever did that had identified the driver as Herbert Ball Shea, it wouldn't be hard to guess a possible motive, would it?"

Ryan looked away and said nothing.

"So...what my brother and I would like to know is whether the man known in Coldwater as Herbert Ball was known elsewhere or previously as Herbert Ball Shea? Was he a shareholder, directly or indirectly, under either name or any corporate name in the Coldwater Bank? And did he fund, in whole or in part, directly or indirectly, the purchase of the assets of the former Coldwater Savings and Loan—presumably out of his ill-gotten gains from advising 'linked financing' brokers during the 1980s savings and loan crisis?"

Ryan's eyes remained closed, and his tongue mute, but his breath came loud and fast. The edge of his thinning hairline beaded with sweat. "What do you want?" he whispered.

"The information I asked for. Information that might establish a motive for someone to run Herbert Ball Shea off the road, killing him and my mother."

Ryan looked sick.

"Neither my brother nor I have an interest in exposing what you or Herbert Ball Shea may have done back in the day. Our only interest is in finding out who killed our mother. But let me be clear, Andrew. You are going to help. Or the scope of the Morgan brothers' interest will expand in a direction you're likely to find uncomfortable."

* * *

Joe sat in the back booth at Trudy's diner looking like ten miles of hard road. His face looked pale, and it stretched tight with pain. What was left of a burger and fries congealed on his plate.

"I thought you were checking yourself back into the hospital," said Tom.

"I did." Joe pulled a vial of pills from his pocket. "They patched me back up and gave me this…" he read from the label, "Oxycontin."

"That's some strong stuff, brother."

"Hope so."

A waitress came over and took Tom's order. When she left, he asked, "Since you're not in the hospital, when do you plan to impound Ryan's Mercedes?"

"Don't need to. I took some paint samples last night."

"With a warrant, right? We don't want mom's killer getting off on a technicality."

"Don't start with me, Tommy. What did you get from Andrew Ryan?"

Tom folded his hands on top of the Formica table. "Confirmation that mom's boyfriend was a disbarred lawyer named Herbert Ball Shea and that our hometown bank was funded, in part, by his and Andrew Ryan's ill-gotten gains during the 1980s savings and loan crisis. That there are more than a few people who might relish an opportunity to ram Herbert Ball Shea from behind. But nothing to tell us who did."

"Assuming whoever did it knew it was Herbert behind the wheel of my truck."

"That's right. The most likely scenario is still that someone was after you. It was your vehicle, hit from behind at night, the one and only time anybody but you was driving it. I doubt anyone would have recognized an eighty-year-old Herbert Ball Shea under those conditions or seized the unexpected opportunity to run him off the road."

"But somebody trashed mom's apartment looking for something. And they, or someone else, went through Herbert Ball's place. I don't believe in coincidences, Tommy. And I don't think Herbert's glasses walked out of Mom's apartment on their own after he was dead."

"So they were Herbert's glasses? You didn't say that before."

"I don't know. They were old fart glasses. Wire rims."

"Okay. I can't really place that as a clue. But what's your next step?"

"Depends on what those paint samples show. I should have them tomorrow."

"And if it's not a match?"

"Something will come up."

Tom recalled the first time he'd shot a deer with a bow and arrow. It was a lethal shot, well placed. But the buck was huge, and the wound not immediately fatal. When the wide-antlered animal disappeared into the dense woods, Tom and his dad tracked it until the trail faded and there were no more flecks of blood, broken twigs, or crushed leaves. After that, they walked in concentric circles from the last sign, heads down, expanding the range by ten yards each time. When it got dark, MadDog lit a Coleman lantern, and they continued the search by lamplight. Then it began to rain. A half-hour later, he ended the search. "I'm sorry, Tommy. No hunter likes to give up the trail and leave a dead animal in the woods for the coyotes to find. But when there's nothing left to go on, that's all you can do. It hurts. But you have to know when it's time to go home."

Tom looked at his brother. "I can't stay, Joe. I found the Ryan and Bell/Shea connection. If the paint sample comes back a match, you've got your killer, too. If it doesn't, then whoever ran your truck off the road was most likely after you, not Mom or Herbert Bell Shea. Either way, there's nothing left for me to do here that you can't do yourself as well or better."

"So, you're punking out?"

"Call it what you want. But tonight, I'm on a plane."

Chapter Fifteen

Bonnie left the lawyer's office feeling relieved, but indecisive. The lawyer said there should be no problem getting temporary alimony. That took a weight off her mind. At least she and the kids wouldn't be destitute. But he also said that she could not make Joe move out of the house. Joe had as much right to live in the jointly owned family home as she and the children. She could, if she wanted to, move out and find another place. But the court would calculate the amount of temporary alimony based on the assumption that she and the children would be staying in the house, husband in residence or not. Joe had no history of violence at home, so there was no basis for an order to vacate.

The lawyer also said that the divorce process could take as long as two years. Longer if custody and visitation became an issue. Bonnie could not imagine staying under the same roof with an angry Joe for that long. She could not imagine staying under the same roof with him for one night, once he'd been served papers. She didn't want to be anywhere near him then. He was still in jail, thank God. But once he got out, then what?

As soon as Bonnie got home, she poured herself a drink and went to sit on the back porch and stare at the lake. Go or stay? She looked at her phone. Call Mom and Dad? Call Mark? No, he's already suffered enough on my account. Joe might actually kill him this time. The decisions she needed to make were coming too fast. She wasn't ready. But the unavoidable truth was that her human volcano of a husband would be home soon. She couldn't be here for that. Counseling had not changed him, nor was there any hope. Mary had been right. Joe was who he was and he would never change.

You can't stay.

Luke had ridden his bike to school and would be home soon. Meghan and Kate would finish with soccer practice in another hour. Bonnie roused herself to pack a bag for each and put them in the back of the Mountaineer. *But where do I take them? To a hotel? To Mom and Dad's? Decide!*

As she continued to dither, Luke rode up the gravel drive on his bicycle. He looked at the car and at the bags inside and then at his mother. "We're going to visit Grandma and Grandpa," she explained. Luke shook his head. "It's just for a while, honey. Until things settle down." He shook his head again, this time forcefully. "Put your bike in the shed. We're going to pick up your sisters at soccer practice."

Luke picked up his bicycle. But instead of walking it to the shed, he spun it around and peddled fast toward town.

Bonnie got into the Mountaineer, intending to catch up with her son. *What am I going to do when I catch up with him? Manhandle him into the car?* She was pretty sure that she couldn't do that. Not yet an adolescent, Luke had nevertheless the beginnings of his father's strength, if not yet his size.

While she fretted over what to do – about Luke, the girls, her life, and even the next few minutes, her phone rang. *What fresh hell...?* She pressed the phone to her ear.

"Mrs. Morgan, this is Trooper Grogan. I'm sending an officer out to your house this afternoon to talk to your son."

"He's not here, Paulie."

"When do you expect him back?"

"I don't know. But we're leaving as soon as he does. I'm taking the children to my parents. We can't be here when you release Joe. I don't feel safe."

There was a momentary pause. Then, "Mrs. Morgan, your husband was released on bail within hours of his arrest."

"What?"

"And your son is a material witness to an attempted murder. He may even be a suspect. You must not remove him from the jurisdiction."

"A suspect! Paulie, what are you talking about?"

"I'm sending a trooper to your house right now, Mrs. Morgan. Please don't leave. It is not in your son's best interest."

Bonnie held the phone in front of her face, stared at it, and then hung up.

* * *

Luke left his bike outside the two-story, red brick town hall building and went downstairs to the sheriff's office to look for his dad. A man dressed in a light gray uniform and black clip-on tie looked up from the desk where his dad usually sat. "That was quick," he said. "Is your mother outside?" Luke shook his head. "Okay. Have a seat." The man pointed to the wooden chair beside the desk. Luke looked around for his dad but didn't see him. The man walked over to a metal cabinet and retrieved a large plastic bag marked "Evidence." He removed a bow and quiver from it and asked in a low, soft voice, "Is this yours?" Luke nodded. The man continued to stare without breaking eye contact. "Did you use this to shoot your father?" Luke looked at the quiver with the missing arrow, felt his body begin to tremble, and then bolted for the door.

* * *

Joe made one stop after leaving Trudy's diner and then drove home. He didn't know what to expect when he got there. But as far as he was concerned, his holier-than-thou wife had some explaining to do. Who was that guy at church? And where did he get off playing Knight to the rescue? Joe pulled Herbert's Buick next to the car shed where he found Bonnie sitting behind the wheel of her SUV, staring blank-faced at her phone. Four suitcases lay piled in the back. He got out of the Buick and yanked open the driver's side door of the SUV. "Where do you think you're going?"

Bonnie gasped and tried to pull the door shut.

"Where are the kids?" he demanded.

She snatched the cell phone from the seat, pressed a button and held the phone to her ear. "We're going to visit my parents," she stammered.

"Like hell you are." While his wife spoke confusion into the phone, Joe walked to the front of the Mountaineer, lifted the hood, and ripped out the spark plug wires.

* * *

"So, we are agreed," said Fulton. "The film futures exchange will be formed in Germany. Each of the three major European distributors represented here will hold an equal one-third interest." He looked around the wood-paneled conference room on the top floor of the Barclay's Bank London headquarters and waited for confirmation.

Karlheinz Klopp was the first to respond. "*Ja,*" he said. "My lawyers have found in Germany the flexible charter company that Mr. Morgan described. We are negotiating with the principals. There will be no issues with the authorities."

"What about start-up funding?" asked Yvette Huppe. "And domain expertise? I agree that the distributors can best control our destinies if we own the exchange rather than sell data to it. But we would be foolish to think we can create a new kind of financial marketplace without additional funding and expert help."

"Barclays will provide the funds," said Fulton. "The companies that provide back-office operations to the stock exchange will want a piece of the build-out. We'll issue an RFP."

"And say what?" asked Madame Huppe.

Fulton opened his mouth. Nothing came out. He looked at Karlheinz Klopp.

"You are having second thoughts?" asked Klopp.

"Not about ownership," said Huppe. "But I have concerns about technology and day-to-day management. None of our businesses involve products and services that Mr. Morgan has described as necessary to compete with traditional bank financing—futures, options, packaged securitizations... Without someone like him, where would we begin?"

Fulton smiled. Klopp drummed his fingers on the table. Huppe spoke again. "One of us must speak with Mr. Morgan."

"And say what?" asked Fulton, repeating her question to him.

"That the distributors would own the exchange but pay him a large fee to make it succeed. Or do any of you have someone in your organization who can do what Mr. Morgan does and not make a mess of it?"

"Barclays will find someone," said Fulton.

"When?" asked Huppe. "People like Mr. Morgan are rare, busy, and expensive. Do any of us want to be negotiating with Hollywood this spring from our current position of weakness?"

Her question was met with silence.

"I must speak with my lawyers," said Klopp.

* * *

Mark Tremblay lay on his back on a narrow frame cot, staring at the timber ceiling. He'd been recuperating in his cousin's hunting cabin in the woods outside of Coldwater for the last two days, pondering what he would do once he healed. The doctors said that the cracked cheek and orbital bones would mend in a month or so. In the meantime, they prescribed rest and no driving. He looked up at the net of cobwebs that covered most of one corner of the ceiling and wondered if this was what they had in mind.

Napping for long stretches of time and taking even longer walks in the woods, he asked himself over and over why he remained on this side of the lake. It was safer on the Canadian side, and medical treatment there was free. Joe Morgan's being anywhere nearby was good enough reason to get out. But...

Be realistic, man. Has she ever said or done anything to encourage your attention? Haven't you made it clear how you would respond if she did? What is there left to do or say? Tremblay's thoughts went round and round while he walked and pondered. But they brought him no closer to understanding or action. Then his phone began to vibrate. The screen flashed her number.

"Bonnie?"

"Mark. Thank God you're still here."

"What's happened?"

"A mess. Joe's been released. I packed the car to get us out of here. But he came home before I could pick the children up at school, and he did something to the car to make it not work. Luke's taken off on his bicycle, and I'm stranded."

"I'll be right there."

"Would you? Are you still in Coldwater?"

"I'm on my way."

Knight to the rescue, or walking face first into a Joe Morgan buzz saw? Tremblay's fantasy pictured it one way, but his gut warned it could be the other. Where could he take them? Not here to his cousin's cabin. Bonnie must have a plan. Maybe she just needed help to get there. Then what?

He climbed into his truck and headed toward Coldwater. Skirting town to avoid being seen or running into anyone named Joe Morgan, he made his way slowly up the switchback dirt and gravel road that led to the Morgan timber mansion. Halfway there, he spotted Bonnie's son, Luke, sitting on the parapet of a stone bridge, throwing rocks into the water. A bicycle with a flat rear tire leaned against the stone wall beside him. Tremblay stopped the truck and rolled the window down. "Need a ride?" Luke looked up and shook his head. "You're not going to get far on that flat tire. Why don't you throw the bike in the back, and I'll take you wherever you need to go." Luke looked at his bicycle, but he didn't move.

"Come on." Tremblay left the truck and hoisted the boy's bicycle onto the flatbed. Luke slid off the stone wall and climbed into the passenger side as Tremblay eased himself behind the wheel. "Where are we going? Home?" The boy didn't answer. He didn't look up. Instead, his eyes fixed on the long-visored cap with a tan neck flap that lay on the bench seat between them. He looked at Tremblay's face. "Don't be frightened by the patch. It's just to keep the dust out."

As Tremblay sought soothing words and a smooth way to get the boy to his mother, Luke began to hyperventilate. He stared at Tremblay, then back at the hunting cap.

Tremblay followed the boy's gaze. He was staring at the hunting cap that Bobby Travis had left in the truck on opening day of archery deer season when he'd borrowed it to go hunting. *Shit.*

Luke stared at Tremblay's face, and his hand reached for the door. Without thinking, Tremblay pressed the door lock button.

You didn't shoot Joe Morgan, did you, Cuz?

The boy yanked on the door handle, then tried to make himself small by squeezing into the corner between the seat and the door. He looked at the hunting cap and then at his own reflection in the truck mirror.

The kid must have seen you, and now he thinks it was me. Did you go looking for Morgan? Or did he just wander by, and you let one fly? Would you do that? Of course, you would.

"I... want... to... go... home," said Luke.

Tremblay looked at the boy. For a while, he didn't move. Then he turned the truck around and drove fast toward his cousin's cabin, having no idea of what he would do once he got there.

Chapter Sixteen

Tom left Trudy's diner with ten hours to kill before he had to board the evening flight to London out of Montreal-Trudeau. Driving north along the lake road, he tried to clear his head. The bits and pieces surrounding Andrew Ryan, Herbert Ball Shea, and the violently trashed and carefully searched apartments were a messy puzzle. But it wasn't obvious that they held an answer to the question of who ran Mary and her boyfriend off the road. Especially, as seemed likely, if whoever rammed Joe's truck from behind assumed it was him behind the wheel. Nor was there any evidence that whoever that might have been was also the person who shot Joe in the back with an arrow. The shooter was obviously not some disgruntled savings and loan investor. Maybe he could have a look around the woods where Joe had been shot. Paulie Grogan wasn't doing much investigating, either of the shooting or the hit and run. It might be worth a look around, and would kill a few hours.

Leaving the rental car in a rutted pull-off near the base of Watermelon Hill, he headed off into the woods, trusting ancient memory to lead him to MadDog's old tree stand. The area was public land. But years ago, MadDog had built an illegal tree stand in the middle of a gully of thorn bushes, where only a deer or a masochist would think of going. His sons had learned to shoot from that stand, both with gun and bow and arrow. The site had accounted for a lot of venison over the years.

Originally well hidden, the stand was easy to locate now. The thorn gully had been hacked to stubble, and the ground cover for fifty yards in every direction had been trampled flat. When Tom got to the stand, he placed his hands and feet on the black metal pegs that had been screwed into either side of the tree and climbed until he reached the narrow, camouflaged platform. Even with the gully hacked and the ground cover flattened, there was no clear shooting lane from the platform through the surrounding trees much longer than forty yards in any direction. Behind the stand rose a thick wall of white pine that no arrow could have penetrated on a straight line. Neither Luke nor anyone else could have shot in a straight line from here in any direction other than straight down the gully.

Tom left the stand and began to walk the few clear shooting lanes. Fifty yards downhill, a perimeter of yellow police tape surrounded a patch of dried blood. From there, an army of boot prints led through a trampled thicket of burdock to another perimeter of yellow tape about fifty yards west of the first. More dried blood stained the ground inside the second taped perimeter. None led out of it except in the direction of the tree stand. *So, this is where you almost bought it, brother.*

A trampled maze of boot prints led back toward the illegal tree stand, and almost as many ran in random diagonals downhill from there. But there were almost no prints or trampled brush heading uphill. *Lazy bastards.* If this was where Joe was shot, the arrow could not have come from the tree stand. Even if Luke had left the stand and stalked his father – a possibility that had undoubtedly occurred to everyone, even if no one would give it voice – the boy would have had to remain unseen, unheard and have found a clear shooting lane where an arrow would not have been deflected by trees, brush or saplings. Tom looked around. There were several clear lanes on the uphill side. But if the arrow came from any of them and passed through Joe, it would have landed no farther than about forty yards downhill. From the myriad boot prints, it was clear that the ground in that direction had been thoroughly searched. Uphill from the taped perimeter, there were only two clear lanes and almost no disturbed ground. Tom walked them both, pausing from time to time to scan the hillside.

Downhill from the stand, most of the ground cover had been trampled nearly to dust. But what remained crackled beneath Tom's feet like woodland alarm bells. *If it was as dry then as it is now, no one snuck up on anyone here.*

He gazed uphill, wondering how far an arrow might have traveled after passing through his brother's thick hide. He walked downhill until the yellow tape was out of sight. From there, an arrow passing through a man at approximately waist high might have gone seventy yards, if it didn't hit a tree first. He turned around and started to walk in that direction.

He didn't spot anything along the first clear lane. Though an arrow passing through there might have been deflected or have buried itself under the loam. A metal detector would have found any arrow buried under ground cover, if it was there. Grogan's searchers, looking for a metal-tipped hunting arrow, had surely thought to bring metal detectors, even if it was obvious that they had not gone far in any uphill direction. Thirty yards above the yellow tape, the ground cover remained untrampled. Retracing his steps, Tom entered the second downhill lane, stopping when the yellow tape was no longer visible. A shot from here could not have gone straight uphill. But there was a narrow lane roughly twenty-five degrees west. He started to walk in that direction.

The shattered arrow lay at the foot of a fat sugar maple about sixty yards diagonally uphill from the yellow tape. Embedded in the tree a few feet above the broken fragment was a bent one-inch broadhead. Tom lifted the arrow by its shattered end, avoiding the shaft and nock that the shooter would have touched. When he held the broken arrow next to his outstretched arm, it reached nearly to his shoulder. It was man-sized, not boy-sized.

* * *

He tried to call Joe from the woods but could not get a signal. When he tried again on the way into town, he saw that his phone battery was dead. A half mile past the volunteer firehouse, he turned into the parking lot of the Coldwater Public Library, hoping it would have a public charger and copies of the last two weeks' *Coldwater Gazette*.

There was no public library in Coldwater when Tom and Joe were kids, nor any store that sold books. But there was a small room above Erickson's ice cream parlor where Mrs. Erickson kept a few books that she lent out on the honor system. Coldwater still didn't have a bookstore. Though a few years ago, the county received federal grant money to build a small public library on the empty lot where the A&P used to be. The owner and publisher of the Coldwater Gazette kept the library supplied with copies of his weekly publication as well as sundry business periodicals that hardly anyone read. Tom stopped at the reception desk to ask if they had a phone charger and if the Coldwater Gazette still carried a daily weather report.

The woman behind the desk smiled and said, "Hello, Tommy Morgan."

One of the many challenges of being an infrequent adult visitor to one's childhood home is the inability to recognize people you haven't seen in twenty years, some of whom may not have finished growing the last time you crossed paths. The smooth-faced companions of his schoolyard adventures, now bearded, balding, or going gray, sometimes taller and inevitably heavier, were impossible to recognize. The girls were a little easier. Most had stopped growing by the end of high school, if not sooner. If their figures were a bit fuller now, hair color was usually consistent with stored memory. But the woman behind the front desk was too young to have been a classmate. And none of his childhood buddies had a younger sister with that rose-colored shade of hair. The woman laughed. "You don't remember me."

Tom smiled and shook his head. "I'm sorry. But all I can be certain of is that you're too young for us to have had a hot date back in the day."

She held out her hand. "Sarah Erickson."

Tom cocked his head. "Sarah, of the braids and banana splits behind the counter of your mom's ice cream shop?"

"And lending library. Do you know you still have overdue books?"

"Ha! How is Mrs. Erickson?"

"She and Dad moved to Florida. I'll have to tell her Tommy Morgan, the notorious book hoarder, stopped by to see her and that I made him leave his bag behind the counter."

"Ouch!" He might have enjoyed a few more minutes of innocent banter if only to keep his hand in. But in the end, he had to collect the weather reports he had come for. He forgot about the charger.

On the way to Joe's office, he found himself reflecting on the quarter-century age difference between the two women he had casually flirted with this week. *You need a life, Tommy Morgan. There's nothing charming about an aging bachelor who thinks he's still got it.*

* * *

When he arrived at Joe's office, Trooper Grogan was sitting behind Joe's desk with his feet on the scarred wood, pretending to solve a crime. Tom recognized him as the uniformed officer who had hauled Joe away at Mary's funeral. He knew the man by reputation, but they had never met. This might not be easy.

Tom held the tip of the bloody arrow between thumb and forefinger and displayed it to the state trooper. "I found this in the woods near where Sheriff Morgan was shot. I thought it might help your investigation. I'm Sheriff Morgan's brother. "

Grogan's head moved slowly in Tom's direction with a look that was less gratitude and more like sizing up a possible opportunity for indoor Taser practice. "You're that lawyer."

"That's right." Tom dismissed the fake lethargy, but not the genuine sneer. "And I believe this is the arrow that skewered my brother. Or what's left of it."

Grogan didn't move. "Believe?"

Tom explained where and how he found it.

"It's hunting season, Morgan. That's probably deer blood."

Already, Tom didn't like the smarmy punk, and he could see that he would have to lean harder. "But you're going to test it for blood type and fingerprints. Right?"

"No."

He had heard the man was a lazy prick. But in Tom's experience, bullies who got their courage from a badge, title, or other substitutes for power always caved when you bullied them back.

"And I'd advise you," the trooper continued, "not to trespass on a crime scene under active investigation, or you'll be spending time back there."

Grogan jerked his head in the direction of the cells. "You and your brother could share a bunk."

Tom stared at Grogan until the trooper blinked. "Fine. If you're not interested, I'll just take it over to the Gazette, tell Jack Thompson where and how I found it when the state troopers couldn't, and how their leader declined to test the bloody arrow for the Coldwater sheriff's blood and the shooter's fingerprints. I'm guessing Jack will find that story newsworthy. If it's a slow week, he might even put your picture on the front page."

Grogan called to the other trooper, whose suppressed grin made clear that he enjoyed watching his boss get schooled by a civilian. "Put this thing in a bag." He turned to Tom, "Anything else?"

"Two things. If that's Sheriff Morgan's blood and there are no prints on the shaft or nock, then whoever shot him knew where Joe might be that day and was there waiting for him."

"Speculation."

"Reasonable deduction. The last time it rained in Coldwater was two weeks before the opening of archery season. I've checked. Davy Crockett couldn't sneak up on Helen Keller in the woods around here when they get dry like that in the fall. But a hunter who had a beef with Sheriff Morgan might let an arrow fly if he happened to be sitting quietly in his favorite hunting spot when the Sheriff walked by instead of a deer. Why not? All the shooter had to do was recover the arrow, and there would be no evidence to link him to the shooting. What our shooter didn't count on was the Sheriff's son being nearby. As soon as the shooter saw the boy running toward the commotion, or the boy saw him, it was time to get out of Dodge. No time to retrieve the evidence. If that's the Sheriff's blood and it was an opportunistic shooting, there'll be prints. If not, it was an ambush."

"More speculation."

"Call it what you want. But bow hunters have to be able to hit a target the size of a pie plate out to forty yards or more..."

Grogan interrupted, "You don't have to tell me how to shoot a bow and arrow, Morgan. I grew up around here."

"Then you know that no one who's practiced enough to do that is going to use a brand-new arrow out of the box on opening day. He'll use the arrows he's practiced with that he knows fly true every time. No prints on a used arrow mean that the shooter wiped the arrow before shooting. No prints on the nock may mean he wore gloves, as well. But it wasn't glove weather. So, no prints means premeditated."

Grogan grunted, "Or your nephew is as ruthless as his father."

"What?"

"You heard me. We know he was there. We recovered his bow near the shooting site, and there's an arrow missing from the quiver. When I asked him point blank if he'd shot his dad, he ran out that door." Grogan lifted his chin. "That says guilty to me."

Tom took a moment to process Grogan's revelation. *Poor Luke, what's going on inside your head, little buddy? What did you see?* To Grogan, he said, "That arrow fragment is almost thirty inches long. That's a man's draw length, not a boy's. And I found it within bow range of where my brother was shot."

"The arrow fragment with the deer blood?" Grogan yawned. "It's men who shoot deer around here, Morgan. Unless your father happens to be the Coldwater Sheriff, and he lets you hunt big game before you're old enough for a license."

Tom looked hard at the state trooper. "I'll share your thoughts on my brother's parenting when I see him. In the meantime, get this thing tested. If the blood is Joe's, the shooter's an adult. And in case you want to look for it, the broadhead and stub that goes with this are still out in the woods. Probably close to where I found this. Both will have blood. And either one could have prints."

Chapter Seventeen

Bonnie stared through the Mitsubishi's windshield at the raised hood, the ripped-out spark plug cables, and at her daughters walking hand in hand up the gravel drive. *Snap out of it.*

The girls spotted the car and slowed their pace. "Where were you, Mom? What happened to the car?" Meghan, the oldest and most difficult to fool, looked at the ripped-out spark plug cables and at the suitcases in the back of the SUV.

"We're going away for a few days," Bonnie explained.

"But we have a soccer match on Saturday!" Kate blurted.

"I know, honey. I'm sorry. But we have to leave. Please go inside and fix yourselves a snack. I have to make a phone call before we leave."

When the girls were out of earshot, Bonnie plucked the phone from the dashboard and dialed Mark Tremblay. He should have gotten here by now. The phone rang several times, but no one answered.

They had to leave. Joe had never been violent at home before. But the look on his face as he tore the wires out of her car was not that of the loving husband and protective father he had once been. He had crossed some kind of line. She was afraid of him now. They had to get away.

But where was Luke? He had taken off so abruptly. Normally, he would be home by dark, no matter what. He'd never been out later than that. But she and the girls could not stay and wait for him. Not with Joe liable to come home at any moment and do God knows what. She looked at the phone and then at Kate and Meghan standing together outside the kitchen door. They looked scared, too. Bonnie punched another number into the phone and listened to it disappear into the black hole of her brother-in-law's voicemail. But instead of hanging up, as she had become used to, in a strained, choppy voice, she blurted, "Tom. It's me. Your brother just ripped some wires out of my car to stop me and the kids from leaving. I'm scared. Do I call the police…? I mean, the state troopers? We have to get out of here, Tom. Tom? Answer your goddamn phone!"

Bonnie looked at the girls still standing anxiously side by side. Then she looked again at her phone and then pressed the number for Paulie Grogan. As soon as the line opened, she began to talk, and she continued until she ran out of breath. "He destroyed one of the cars. Luke ran off. The girls and I are stranded here. I don't know what he might do when he gets back. We're not safe…"

The voice at the other end of the phone oozed a trained calm. Bonnie could hear the sound of pen scratching paper. It was somehow reassuring. "Who has destroyed your car, Mrs. Morgan?"

"My husband. Joe Morgan! He's out of control."

"Hold on." She could hear Grogan talking to someone before getting back on the line. "Mrs. Morgan? Trooper Mulvey is on his way. Who is there, exactly?"

Bonne paused to catch her breath. "Me. My two daughters."

"And where is your son?"

"I don't know. He took off on his bicycle."

"Could he be with your husband?"

Bonnie felt an invisible hand close around her heart. "I don't know. Yes, maybe."

"Do you know if your husband is armed? Was he wearing his gun when he vandalized your car?"

Bonnie closed her eyes and summoned the stark image: eyes flat, smile cold. "Yes. He was wearing his Glock."

* * *

Tom got back to his motel room, plugged his phone into the charger, and discovered that he had half a dozen voicemails. The first two were from Yvette Huppe, asking him to call immediately. The third, a few hours later, was from her, as well. "Tom you must answer your phone. Karlheinz Klopp has taken your idea. His lawyers have found a company in Germany of the kind you described, and Karlheinz would have the distributors buy it. Barclays would provide the start-up financing. Tom, you must return now."

The message from Varné was equally grim. Over the noise of the Tel Aviv airport, the Frenchman's voice sounded rushed and somber. "The Israelis are willing to license their technology," the somber voice on the message said. "But there were only technical people at our meetings. They asked no business questions. I think they cannot be a legitimate business. Perhaps a commercial front for one of the intelligence services. I don't know. But Tom, I cannot help a foreign government put its spy technology into French homes. *La' Sûreté* would never permit. I am desolated."

Shit.

The last message was from Bonnie, and it was an hour old.

"Tom. It's me. Your brother just ripped some wires out of my car to stop me and the kids from leaving. I'm scared. Do I call the police...? I mean, the state troopers? We have to get out of here, Tom. Tom? Answer your goddamn phone!"

What the hell, brother?

Tom left the motel and drove fast toward his brother's lair. When he got there, he found Bonnie's SUV with its hood up and engine wires dangling. She and the kids were gone. He called her number and got her voicemail. "It's me," he said. "I'm at your house, and no one is here. I'll find my brother. Let me know that you and the kids are safe. Call me when you get this."

For God sake, Joe

* * *

Where was Joe? There were only a finite number of possibilities. If he had vandalized his wife's car so that she couldn't leave, he was probably still around. If he thought it was no big deal, he might even have gone to the office. Tom got back into his car and drove toward town, not entirely sure what he was going to say or do when he found his brother. *Son of MadDog. WTF?*

Joe had been driving Herbert Ball's Buick ever since his Silverado got run off the road and totaled. But the only cars Tom saw in the lot behind the sheriff's office were a pair of blue state trooper vehicles spread across three diagonal parking spaces. He parked the rental car a prudent distance away and descended the stone steps to his brother's office. If Joe was there….? What would he say or do, exactly? He didn't know. But there was no choice except to go in and find out.

When he entered the dimly lit office, he found a uniformed state trooper sitting at the front desk playing a video game on his laptop. Paulie Grogan lounged where Tom had left him earlier, feet up on MadDog's old desk. "What can I do for you now, Morgan?" The tone and the hands folded behind the head said as clearly as anything that *Trooper* Grogan had no interest in doing anything for his former boss's brother.

"I'm looking for the sheriff."

"So are we." Grogan dropped his hands and leaned forward across the desk. "His wife filed for a protective order about an hour ago."

Shit.

"We're looking for your nephew, too." Grogan returned his hands to the back of his head and looked hard at Tom. "As a suspect in his father's shooting."

Tom laughed. "He's ten years old!"

"And in possession of a hunting bow in proximity to the shooting site. He fled the scene. We've recovered his weapon. There's an arrow missing."

Tom was of two minds. He needed to find Joe, but failing to stop this fool from pursuing Luke as a suspect in his father's shooting would almost certainly lead to more trouble. "What about that blood-covered, man-sized arrow I gave you? The one that your searchers missed, stuck into a tree just fifty yards in an unobstructed line from the shooting site. Did you get it tested yet?"

Grogan yawned and shook his head. "We've been busy here today, Morgan.

Missing kid. Domestic violence. Deer blood can wait."

Tom struggled to keep his voice calm. "Trooper Grogan, for a filing fee of fifteen dollars I can go upstairs and petition for a writ of mandamus to order you to have that arrow fragment tested. Attached to that writ will be an affidavit as to where and how I found it, how I gave it into your custody, and our conversation about having it tested. That affidavit will become part of the public record available to your bosses, the local newspaper, the mayor's office, and any interested citizen. So, unless you tell me now that you will have that arrow tested today, that's exactly what's going to happen next."

Grogan smirked. "Don't get your undies in a bundle, Morgan."

"Then do it. Now."

The trooper at the front desk suppressed a smile.

Tom left the sheriff's office uncertain of where to go next. Was Grogan even looking for Joe or Luke? They could be sleeping in one of the back cells, for all that lazy fool seemed to know or care. Obviously, the trooper was in no hurry to get the bloody arrow fragment analyzed. *Deer blood. Bullshit.* A fellow law enforcement officer had been ambushed in the woods, and his mother and companion murdered. But all the state investigator seemed to be doing was lounging behind MadDog's old desk, snarling at dust motes. Could Grogan really be that useless? Or, as Joe had claimed, the only thing his former deputy cared about was helping his new bosses achieve their perennial objective of taking over the Coldwater sheriff's department? Short of that, nothing mattered.

And Joe used to call Manhattan a cesspool.

Like a weary hamster on a wonky exercise wheel, Tom stumbled through a litany of questions and hypotheses. Joe and Luke had to be somewhere. Were they together? Did either know that anyone, other than Bonnie, might be looking for them? Where would you go if you needed a place to crash with a ten-year-old boy if you didn't know anyone was looking for you and you weren't running?

He stopped and looked up at the sky. *Home to mother.*

* * *

Tremblay made peanut butter and jelly sandwiches for Luke and himself. Then, while he was eating, he pretended to call the boy's mother. "Mrs. Morgan, this is Mark Tremblay. Your son got a flat tire on his bicycle. I can take him home, but I don't want to leave him there if the house is empty. Please give me a call when you get this. I'll bring him and his bike home or drop him off wherever you'd like."

"There," he said to Luke. "As soon as she calls back, we'll leave."

Luke chewed at the edges of the peanut butter sandwich, but he did not look up or make eye contact.

"Would you like another," Tremblay asked. "Or a Coke. There're a couple in the fridge."

"I want…to go…home."

"Of course. As soon as your mother calls. She and I are friends, you know. That's how I have her phone number."

The boy stared at Tremblay, suspicion plain on his face. "Why…did my dad…hit you?"

Tremblay had not anticipated the question, and he took a moment to think of an answer that would not spook the kid.

"He made a mistake, Luke. I'm an old friend of your mom's from high school. Your dad must have thought I was someone who was bothering her." The boy seemed to go inside himself then. That was okay. But remembering the hunting cap that seemed to have unnerved the kid, he added, "Make yourself another PBJ, if you want. Or chill. I have to make a phone call. I only borrowed that truck outside for the afternoon. The guy who owns it said he might need it to go hunting in the morning."

Luke's head lifted, and his eyes widened. *Bingo.*

"I'll just ask him if I can keep it until your mom calls. Then I'll bring you home."

Tremblay left the boy to his thoughts and stepped outside, satisfied with his extemporaneous fibbing, but uncertain about what to do next. Should he call Bonnie? This time for real? That felt right. There was still time. Everything might still work out.

As he started to punch in Bonnie's number, he heard the sound of a truck grinding in low gear up the dirt logging road that led to the cabin. His heart began to race. *What?* As the sound got closer, he stepped behind a tree. *Don't let it be Joe Morgan.* With his boy in the cabin, Morgan would... Tremblay didn't want to think about the possibilities. He needed to pee.

The sound of the approaching truck came from behind a line of white pine trees. Tremblay wanted to run, but his legs felt anchored to the loam. All he could do was stand motionless, hoping to remain unseen. The truck appeared from behind the pines and began climbing the dirt track. Tremblay stood unmoving as the truck came to a stop directly in front of the pin oak he was trying to hide behind. The driver leaned out the window and shouted. "What are you doing, Cuz?"

It took a moment for Tremblay to catch his breath. He took a dozen steps toward the truck, and when he got there, he leaned on its hood. Bobby Travis got out of the cab and grabbed Tremblay by the arm. "I asked you a question. What are you doing? You look like you just got caught by Joe Morgan humping his wife." Travis laughed. But not for long.

In halting sentences squeezed between waves of nausea, Tremblay recounted the call from Bonnie Morgan, his picking up the run-away Luke, the boy's strange reaction to seeing Bobby's hunting cap in the back seat of the truck, and his spur-of-the-moment decision to take the boy somewhere while he figured out what to do next. His cousin listened, shaking his head slowly while Tremblay spoke. He did not interrupt. But when Tremblay finally finished, Travis stared at the treetops and said, "You stupid, son-of-a bitch. You kidnapped Joe Morgan's kid and brought him to *my* cabin?"

"It'll be alright, Bobby. I'll just call his mom and bring him home if she's there."

"I don't think so."

"I can't keep him, Bobby!"

"You got that right."

"Then what am I supposed to do?"

Bobby Travis growled, "You can start by giving me your phone and getting rid of that goddamn cap. Then sit tight until I get back."

"Where are you going?"

"Somewhere that kid won't see me and where I can think of a way to keep us both from getting skinned alive by Joe Morgan."

"I'll just take him home."

Travis spat. "Are you brain dead? As soon as that kid opens his mouth, Joe Morgan will hunt us down like rabbits. Can handle that?"

Tremblay felt that his cousin was wrong. But, reflecting on his own decisions of the last few hours, he wasn't sure.

"Give me your goddamn phone and stay put until I come back."

Chapter Eighteen

Bobby Travis parked his truck in front of the lakeside VFW and went inside. In the cool semi-darkness, soldiers from Ft. Drum stood afternoon lazy at the long wooden bar. Later, the desert camo would be five deep in front of the beer-stained mahogany, and the crowd would spill out the front door into the gravel parking lot. But now, there were only a half dozen late afternoon drinkers, and Travis was able to find an empty corner table where he could nurse a tall one and figure out how not to get killed by Joe Morgan.

What had his cousin been thinking? Kidnapping Joe Morgan's kid? How was that supposed to end well? For anybody.

Joe Morgan was ten times worse than his old man. The elder Morgan had been all about the money. You could do business with him. Everybody got along, Hellers and Cashins, too, as long as they didn't get up in Morgan's face. Travis's uncle Claude had a sweet thing going in the 80s, bringing stuff across the lake by boat and sometimes over the bridge in someone else's eighteen-wheeler. That didn't happen now. The Mulveys had some kind of arrangement with the younger Morgan. But the Hellers were on his shit list, and Bobby Travis was a Heller on his mother's side.

According to Bobby's dad, even though you could do business with MadDog Morgan, the former sheriff had started to get greedy toward the end. Once, when Travis's dad was in his cups, he told Bobby a story about Morgan and a suitcase full of bank bonds. Pops was vague about the details, and he had not been involved directly. But somehow, a deal involving military ordinance stolen from Fort Drum had gotten royally screwed up, and a suitcase full of bank bonds and a couple of Canucks had gone missing. Everyone figured the Canadians had done a skip. But two years later, when Morgan paid off a chunk of his house, got himself a new truck and started talking about retirement, he was dead within a month. The bonds and the Canucks stayed missing.

Travis sipped his beer and let his mind wander. If MadDog Morgan took those bonds and waited a couple of years to spend a few, what happened to the rest? Pop said there was a whole satchel full. Even after paying down a house and a truck, there would have been plenty left. If MadDog's son knew where they were…

Travis poured a swill of cold beer down his throat. *You haven't got the brains God gave a goose, cousin. But you just might make one of us rich.*

* * *

It was a risky plan. Joe Morgan might show up with guns blazing. And he would surely take revenge later. Travis didn't like the idea of his cousin getting hurt, or dead. But Tremblay had been an idiot, mooning over Joe Morgan's wife, snatching his kid, and bringing him to the family cabin. Someone was going to get hurt. There was no way to avoid that now. But it was not going to be Bobby Travis. *I should get something out of this, too, for my trouble.* He finished his beer, tossed back a shot, and then stopped at the bar to get change before walking past the pool table to the pay phone in the back.

The guy who answered the phone at the sheriff's office wasn't Joe Morgan, didn't know where he was and didn't have his cell phone number. When the cop, or whoever it was, asked who was calling, Travis hung up. Then he fed another quarter into the phone and called his wife. He hadn't planned to play this card yet. But it couldn't be helped now.

The sultry voice that answered the phone could still move him. She knew how to use what God gave her. But if that dumb bitch was stupid enough to stay around after this, she would get what was coming to her. "It's me," he said. "I need Joe Morgan's cell phone number."

"The Coldwater sheriff? Why don't you call the station?"

Travis felt his face shift between grimace and grin and then back again. "I haven't got time for games, bitch. I'll come home and *get* it out of you if that's what you want. Make the last time feel like a birthday spankin'."

The other end of the line remained silent for a long second, then Crystal Travis choked out a phone number. He scribbled it on the wall of the booth just below a crudely carved penis. In an inspired flourish, he added the words, "Call me for a good time." Then he dialed the number.

When Joe Morgan answered, Bobby gave the pitch that he hoped would make him rich, even if it made his cousin dead. "I know where your boy is, Morgan. But you've got something that doesn't belong to you. Something you inherited from your daddy. A lot of somethings."

"Who the hell is this?"

"Never you mind. Just get that sack of what don't belong to you and bring it to where I tell you. Then I'll let you know where you can find your boy."

"My boy's at home, asshole."

"No, he ain't.

* * *

Joe got in the car and drove fast across town. He was not surprised when Bonnie didn't answer her phone. He was just pissed. He was even more pissed when he found a state trooper standing in front of his house, arm outstretched with his palm facing Joe's car. Joe rolled down the window and growled. "What the hell are you doing?"

The trooper put his hand to the butt of the pistol holstered at his hip. "I'm here to ascertain the whereabouts of your son, Sheriff Morgan, and to escort you to the temporary trooper barracks."

"What do you mean 'ascertain the whereabouts of my son."

"Do you know where your son is, Sheriff?"

"He was with his mother when I left this morning."

"And how about this afternoon when you vandalized her car?"

Joe snorted.

"Your wife has filed for a protective order. She and your daughters have been taken to a secure location. We are trying to locate your son. Do you know where he is?"

"No."

"Then I need to ask you to come with me."

"Right." Joe put the car in reverse and stomped on the gas.

* * *

Tom left the sheriff's office and drove toward his mother's condo. On the way, he remembered that he had not yet returned Yvette Huppe's several phone calls. Too much had happened since he met with Joe that morning and made plans to fly back to London that evening: bloody arrows, Luke gone missing, Joe vandalizing Bonnie's car. He had no time for European double-crossers. But the prospect of film distributors owning the futures exchange where they, their suppliers and customers would all need to go for financing was a recipe for disaster. If the idea wasn't killed in its crib, there would be no project to get back to.

Huppe answered on the third ring. "Monsieur Morgan! How considerate of you to call."

"I'm still in the States, Yvette, and I haven't got a lot of time. Whose idea was it to have the foxes own the chicken coop?"

Huppe did not respond immediately. Tom chastised himself for slipping once again into American slang, something he was prone to do when tired or irritated.

"Herr Klopp's lawyers have made the proposal," she said at last. "They said something about not being able to legally protect an idea, only the expression of it."

"Ha!"

"I must tell you, I think they are right. If the distributors do not own the exchange and all have the same financial risk, a single distributor can make mischief by withholding its data."

"Which the exchange can prevent by signing long-term supply contracts with each distributor. Seriously, Yvette, before you get into a room with people trying to reinvent the wheel, pick up the phone and call me."

"You have been unavailable, Thomas."

She was right. But what the hell? His mother had died. No, she had been murdered. What has to happen for a guy to get a day off? He took a deep breath. *Quit whining.* "My apologies," he said, at last. "I'll be back in Europe in a few days."

"Days? That must be too late, Thomas."

Shit.

"And when such long-term contracts expire?" she pressed. "Or when one distributor provides bad or late data? Then what?"

Fair question and I haven't got time to answer it.

"No, Tomas, I believe that the distributors must share equally the risks and rewards of owning the exchange. Otherwise, it can be harmed by one bad actor."

"Yvette,..."

"But we need also a Tom Morgan to get the exchange started," she interrupted. "That, we cannot do ourselves."

He was tired, and part of him wanted to hang up. But he had too much skin in the game, and he could not afford to lose it. "Yvette, you can't do any of it yourselves. You don't have the technical, financial, or regulatory expertise. And each of the distributors has a different agenda, which is incompatible with effective joint ownership. Clement Frères wants to keep its independence. The Brits want to keep the status quo with the UK banks, and Karlheinz Klopp wants to be a big cheese in Europe. If you'll allow me a nautical metaphor, each of your oars is pulling in a different direction. If you try to steer that way, the ship will crash on the first rocks."

"I disagree."

Tom stared at the passing landscape, feeling the weight of cumulative fatigue and impatient disappointment. He was being played, which was no surprise. But he didn't have the time or juice to deal with it.

"So, what does Tom Morgan want?" Yvette demanded.

"For what?"

"For not letting a brilliant and timely idea fail."

He pulled his car into the parking lot in front of his mother's condo and stared through the windshield. The exchange would fail if it launched with the ownership structure the distributors wanted. But he had too much at stake, financially and professionally, to wash his hands of the whole project and wish Madame Huppe and her new partners good luck and good riddance. Even if that's really what he wanted to do. Could there be a fair price for agreeing to pilot a doomed ship? Sure. There was a price for everything.

Not nearly as appalled by his shameless greed as he knew that he should be, he made a proposal certain to cause the distributors to lose their collective breakfasts. Especially when they realized they had no option. "I'll take a ten percent ownership interest in the German company that will ultimately own the exchange. And a ten-year put to the distributors, exercisable at any time, at one times revenues."

He could sense that Huppe was doing the mental arithmetic and not liking the result.

"Karlheinz may…"

"Karlheinz will be as happy as a pig in mud as long as he gets the centerfold of the Financial Times and the cover of *Der Spiegel.* You'll get what *you* want: more quality European film, more patrons, and—at least for now—retained family control. I have no idea what the UK distributors want. But having Fulton lead, and Barclays run the play means that nothing will get done on the UK end. So, the owners had better start lining up additional financing. Fast."

"Or this ship, as you call it, 'will hit the rocks'?"

"With no survivors."

* * *

Tom climbed the steps to his mother's condo and knocked on the front door. When no one answered, he held his thumb to the doorbell. Almost immediately, the door burst inward as if ripped by a passing nor'easter. Behind it stood the Coldwater sheriff, dressed in full camo and wearing a flack vest and a two-handgun shoulder holster strapped to his torso. "You…!"

"Nice to see you, too, brother. Let me in."

"Get lost."

"The state troopers are out looking for you. They think you snatched Luke."

"You're with *Grogan* now?"

"Are you going to let me in?"

"No."

"Fine. I'll call Grogan and let him know you're here. He's looking for Luke, too."

Joe glared. "Get in."

As Tom stepped into his deceased mother's apartment, he couldn't help but recall the 'don't let the door hit you in the butt' sendoff he had received the last time he was in this room when his mother was still alive. He understood more about her now than he did then. But what he knew hardly justified that less-than-maternal dismissal.

He followed Joe past her closed bedroom door and into the galley kitchen beyond. There, spread across the top of the Formica kitchen table, lay half a dozen stacks of what looked like couponed bearer bonds, a leather briefcase, two 9mm Glock handguns, and a 12-gauge double barrel shotgun. As between the weapons and the stacks of bonds, Tom was shocked only by the latter.

Early in his career, he had been involved in several deals where the medium of exchange was bearer bonds. In addition to their legitimate use, bearer bonds had once been the preferred medium of exchange for large criminal transactions. The bonds were as anonymous as cash with several other advantages. Issued in much larger denominations than currency, they also paid interest and carried coupons that could be detached and cashed separately with no questions asked and no requirement for the payer to keep a record of the transaction. The United States government had stopped issuing them in the early 1980s and had made it unlawful for corporations to issue new ones. But it was still legal to possess and exchange the older, lawfully issued ones.

How had little brother come to possess such a haul of them? And what were they doing stacked on Mary Morgan's kitchen table beside a pair of semi-automatic pistols and a double-barreled shotgun?

"I thought I was coming here with good news," said Tom, pointing to the odd and damning tableau on top of the Formica table. "I'm not so sure now."

Joe leaned against the door frame, looking large and lethal. "What good news?"

Tom stepped away from the bonds and weaponry and rested his backside against the kitchen counter. "I found a blood-covered arrow about fifty yards uphill from where you were shot. I gave it to Paulie Grogan to test for blood type and prints. He prefers to believe that your underage hunting companion shot you. Even after I pointed out that the arrow I found is man-sized, not boy-sized."

"Paulie Grogan is a lazy idiot."

"Who is lazily looking for you and Luke, who, he theorizes, you abducted."

Joe shoveled the stacks of bonds into an open leather satchel, scooped up the briefcase, pistols, and shotgun, and headed for the door."

"Where are you going?"

"None of your business."

"Fine. I'll just call Grogan now." Tom took his cell phone from his pocket and started to scroll for a number.

Joe raised one of the Glocks and pointed it at Tom's chest. "Luke isn't here, as you can see for yourself. I'm going to get him."

Tom gestured at the guns. "And you need all that."

"Yes."

"Then I'm coming with you." The words came out of Tom's mouth without thought or hesitation, which was surely a sub-optimal way to make decisions involving weapons and his brother.

"No."

"Then I'm calling for trooper backup."

Joe glowered. "Tommy, I haven't got time for your smart-ass bullshit. Get out of my way unless you want the crap beaten out of you again. I think you would have had enough of that by now."

Tom put up his hands and stepped backward. Joe snorted and brushed him aside. As he passed, Tom lifted the nearest kitchen chair and brought it down hard on his brother's head.

* * *

When Joe regained consciousness, he was looking at the barrel of a 12-gauge shotgun aimed at his crotch. "Where's Luke?" Tom asked.

Joe propped an elbow under his torso and made as if to get up.

"Don't move."

"Eat shit, lawyer boy. You're not going to kill me."

"You're right. I'm going to emasculate you. Look at where this is pointing and then answer my question. Where's Luke?"

"You don't have the balls."

"You can join the club."

Joe reached a hand to the back of his head. "I haven't got time for this, Tommy. I don't know where he is."

Tom clicked off the trigger safety next to the right side gun barrel. The left one was already off.

Joe sniggered, "You got more of the old man in you than I thought."

"Stop thinking. Start talking."

"Alright, listen good. Because I haven't got time for this. I found a footlocker of those bonds in the attic of our old house when I moved Mom into the Senior Center. When I asked her about it, all she would say was, 'They're your father's.' Then, about two hours ago, I got a phone call from someone who claims to have Luke and who knew about MadDog's stash." Joe pointed to the open satchel. "That's what he wants in exchange for Luke."

Tom blew a short, sharp breath. "Some local glue sniffer kidnapped Luke, and you haven't called the BCI or the feds?!"

"Tommy, I could give a shit about the old man's retirement fund. But I can't get the BCI or the feds involved. This is unfinished family business, and it has to stay that way."

"Says who?"

"Says common sense. What do you think paid for your college and law school? Or Mom's condo. Or Luke's medical bills?"

And that log mansion on ten acres you call home? "I borrowed for law school," said Tom.

"Good for you. Government subsidized, low interest, no collateral, pay back whenever. But did you ever think about the rest of it? Did you ever ask?"

"Where is Luke?" Tom repeated, although this time he was stalling.

"Wherever this guy's got him." Joe looked at the digital clock over the microwave oven. "The meet is in a half hour. So, either blow my balls off, get out of my way, or make yourself useful. I'm leaving."

Tom put the shotgun down. "We'll take my car. The state troopers are looking for yours."

Chapter Nineteen

Joe put the satchel of bonds, briefcase, and a large cardboard box in the trunk of Tom's car. Then he laid the shotgun across the back seat and covered it with a dark towel. Anyone who looked closely through the window could have spotted the shoulder-holstered Glocks. But they would have had to know what they were looking at. "Where are we going?" Tom asked.

"Twelve miles up the lake road. Then look for a broken telephone pole." They drove in silence for several minutes, enough time for Tom to start second-guessing what they might be about to do. Joe looked over at him several times before finally breaking the silence. "So, tell me about those high-class English girls who all talk like Lady Di."

"What?"

"You getting any peaches and cream?"

Tom didn't think himself easily shocked. But, as he and Joe were heading toward something that might require the use of weapons, he would have preferred that Joe remain focused on strategy and tactics rather than fantasies about fair English maidens. "Are you serious?" he sputtered. "Get your head into whatever game this is we're in! Your son's just been kidnapped on account of the Morgan family hustle of enrichment through law enforcement that got his grandfather killed and maybe even his grandmother. If we have to use that arsenal you brought, it might just kill you, me and Luke, as well."

Joe snorted.

"I mean it, brother." Tom slowed the car and pulled off on the side of the road. "This has got to stop."

"What are you doing?"

Tom turned off the engine and faced his brother. "Thinking about your son, for God's sake. It's one thing if you don't walk out of this. But Luke? Are you seriously going to risk *his* life just to keep the secret of how the Morgan family made its ill-gotten gains? It's not as if the whole town doesn't know that MadDog was crooked."

Joe put his hand around the butt of the Glock and drew it from his holster. "I haven't got time for this, Tommy."

Tom reached for the car keys. Joe slammed Tom's head hard into the steering column. When Tom regained consciousness, Joe was behind the wheel of the car, and they were moving slowly down a dark, overgrown track surrounded by thick pine trees. "Don't," was all Joe said when he saw that Tom was awake. "Don't even think about it."

When they came to a fork in the track, Joe got out of the car, opened the trunk and took out the leather briefcase and the cardboard box. Then he dropped the leather briefcase into Tom's lap through the open window of the passenger side door. "Look through this while I take care of something. It was in the trunk of Herbert's car." He picked up the cardboard box and started down the fork of the track they had not taken. Tom watched him in the rearview mirror until he disappeared.

Blood covered the front of Tom's shirt, and his nose felt squishy to the touch. He had no idea what to expect next and no way to plan for it. But with nothing to do until Joe got back, he tried to distract himself from the throbbing in his face by going through the contents of Herbert Ball's briefcase: two passports, one American in the name of Herbert Ball, the other Canadian in the name of Herbert Ball Shea, and a slim cardboard file labeled: Coldwater Bank. In the file were copies of the bank's board of directors meetings for the last two years. As Tom read through them, one by one, the list of who might have wanted Herbert Ball dead and why grew longer.

When Joe returned to the car, he lifted the shotgun and Glocks from the back seat and strapped on the handgun holsters.

"What were you doing back there?" asked Tom.

"Luke leaves with us. Or whoever took him is not going anywhere."

Tom's head throbbed and his face ached. It was too much to process.

"I swear, the whole Heller clan is brain-dead," Joe muttered. "They've had a cabin down this road for over fifty years. Do they think I don't know about it? That's where they must have taken Luke. Down the other way, where the guy said to meet, is a trash dump. He's probably got a surprise party waiting there."

* * *

The cabin was hidden at the end of a narrow ravine, accessed by a footpath through thickets of thorn and burdock. Built of lodge pole spruce and chinked with mud and clay, it may once have had a pine shingle roof. Now, the roof was covered by patches of green moss grown thick over strips of faded tar paper. Joe pointed to the wisp of smoke rising from the stone chimney and two figures visible through the cracked window. "I'll go in," said Tom.

"No. They're expecting me."

Tom pointed to the weapon in his brother's hand and the ones strapped across his chest. "Are they expecting that, too?"

Joe handed the shotgun and one of the handguns to Tom and tucked the other into the back of his waistband.

"What do you want me to do if you run into trouble?" Tom asked.

"Shoot everyone not named Morgan."

Tom looked at the shotgun and sidearm. "I haven't fired a side-by-side since we were kids, Joe. And this handgun looks like something out of Star Wars. Where's the safety? And the hammer?"

"It doesn't have either."

Tom handed the weapons back. "You don't want me trying to figure out modern police weaponry in the middle of a gunfight with your son in the line of fire. Just give me the bonds. I'll get Luke."

"Some backup." Joe took back the weapons and handed the satchel of bonds to Tom. "Give them this shit, grab Luke and walk out of there. No chit-chat. If you're not out in three minutes, I'm coming in."

Tom took the leather satchel and started across a clearing of sharp rock and tufted weeds, his heart beating like a paddle wheel. He tried not to stumble. At the cabin door, he knocked and waited, hearing the sound of scraping chairs and muffled voices inside. A man who looked more like a schoolteacher than a kidnapper opened the door. Tom felt there was something familiar about him, but he couldn't say what. The man's hands twitched, and his face spread in surprise. When he didn't speak, Tom stepped into the cabin and held the satchel at arm's length. "Here it is."

"What? Who are you?"

"It's what you asked for. I'm the boy's uncle. Where is he?"

The man seemed confused.

"Uncle Tom!" Luke jumped from the slat bed in the corner of the room, pushed his way past the man, and threw his arms around Tom's waist.

"Hey buddy, you okay?"

Luke held tight but said nothing more.

Tom looked over Luke's head at the kidnapper. "You want to check that? Count it? Or can we leave?"

The man looked uncertain and scared. "What is it?"

"What you asked for, or so I was told."

"I didn't ask for anything. The boy's bicycle broke down."

Tom looked at him in disbelief. "Twelve miles from town? In the middle of the woods?"

"No. No. I can explain. I'm a friend of the boy's mother. My name is Mark Tremblay."

Tom held up his hand, stepped to the door, and waved to the spot across the clearing where he had left Joe. Luke kept his grip around Tom's waist. Joe hustled across the clearing, shotgun angled across his chest. As he got close to the cabin, his eyes bore into the face of the man standing behind Luke. "You?!" he shouted.

"Joe…Sheriff…the boy's bicycle had a flat…there was no one home…I wasn't thinking…"

Joe looked from the kidnapper to Tom and back to the kidnapper again. Then he lifted the shotgun.

CHAPTER NINETEEN

"BOOM!

An explosion like a quarry blast shook the trees beyond the clearing, followed by the smell of smoke and gasoline. Joe threw the shotgun to Tom and ran toward the blast.

"What? What's happening?" asked Tremblay.

"Do you have friends out there?" Tom asked.

"No. I mean, yes. This is my cousin's cabin. I've just been staying here."

Other than his initial shout of "Uncle Tom!" Luke had not said a word. Tom walked the boy to the back of the cabin and told him to sit on the floor away from the door and window. "You'd better keep away from there, too," he told Tremblay.

"No. I mean, I should go see."

Tom pointed to the satchel of bonds on the floor by the cabin door. "You want to take that?"

"What is it?"

"You don't know?"

"No. I shouldn't even be here. I mean, I should, I'm staying here. But I shouldn't have brought the boy. His mother… his mother wasn't home. The bicycle was broken." Tremblay shook his head, muttering. "I couldn't bring him to his father…" The man looked at Luke, as if for understanding, and then he looked at Tom. "I did call…" He started for the door.

"Where are you going?"

The man looked at Tom. Gunfire erupted from the woods.

"Get away from that door," said Tom. "Who owns this place?"

Tremblay moved toward the window. "My family. My cousin's family."

"Get away from there, too." The gunfire came from two different places. It wasn't just Joe shooting. "Is your cousin a Heller?"

Tremblay shook his head. "A Travis."

"They're related, aren't they?"

Tremblay spread his hands. "I guess. On his mother's side."

"What about you?"

Tremblay shook his head and moved toward the door. "I should go."

Tom scoffed. "Go where? There're two guys out there shooting at each other. They'll shoot you, too, if you step out that door. One on general principle and the other to keep your mouth shut."

* * *

Bobby Travis sat with his back against a thick pine tree, listening for the snap of twig, rustle of leaves, or other telltale sound of pursuit. After a few long minutes, he made his way toward the car he had seen parked at the end of the dirt track. It wasn't Joe Morgan's car; Travis knew that one well. But Morgan had obviously come in it. When Travis got to the car, he ripped his undershirt into strips, opened the gas tank, and stuffed the tied-together strips into the tank with a stick. When the cloth had soaked enough gas to wick as far as the tank opening, he untied a shorter piece and wrapped it around the end of the stick he had used to shove the shirt strips into the tank. Then he lit the end of the gasoline-soaked cloth that hung out of the tank, ran into the woods, and waited for the explosion. He didn't have to wait long.

BOOM!

"Back atcha!" Travis chuckled. Morgan's booby trap had blown the rear tires off Travis's Ford 150. But the homemade explosive device wasn't large enough to do more damage than that. Now Morgan was stranded, and the odds were now even, maybe better. Morgan would have to go to the cabin to get his kid. Or maybe he was there already. Either way, Joe Morgan was now the hunted.

* * *

Joe watched the man he'd been chasing approach the cabin carrying a stick wrapped in dirty white cloth and then disappear around back. Tommy and Luke were still inside with that gibbering fool who had approached Bonnie at Mary's funeral. Or maybe he'd left already. If so, he wouldn't get far. The only way out was on foot.

As Joe watched the cabin, a wisp of chimney smoke appeared to spread across the back of the roof. Then, the guy who had disappeared behind the cabin appeared at the edge of the clearing, beyond the range of Joe's handguns. Joe watched him watching the door of the cabin. When the roof began to smolder, Joe slipped quietly into the woods, running silently toward the man who was now pointing a handgun at the cabin's only exit.

* * *

Tom heard the cackle of the flames and smelled the smoke. They all did. Scanning the room for what might be used to put out a fire, or to escape one, he pointed to the slat table in the center of the room. "Help me with that," he said.

"What's going on?" gasped Tremblay.

"Luke, you help, too. We've got to break off those legs."

Tom flipped the table on its side and put his weight on the nearest leg, snapping it off at the corner joint. He did the same to the other leg and then pushed the table toward the floor, snapping the last two. Then he shouted at Tremblay. "YOU! Help me lift this. We're going out that door behind it. Don't let go or drop it until we reach the woods."

"I...I..."

"Jesus, man. Do you want to fry!"

Tom slid the broken table toward the door and then propped it upright on its side. "Luke, get behind me." Tom eased the door open and waited for the shot. When it didn't come, he shouted to Tremblay, "Get over here, man. Grab that broken stub." Tremblay stumbled forward and locked both hands around the broken top right table leg. Tom put his hand under the leg stub on the opposite side. "Luke, hold onto my belt." The boy nodded and came forward, gripping Tom's belt from behind. "On three," Tom shouted. "Lift and run. One. Two. Three!" Tom and Tremblay lifted the table, and the two men and the boy ran through the open door, holding the table in front of them like a shield. The woods to their left erupted in gunfire.

* * *

Joe was in position. When the door to the cabin burst open and the man who'd been watching it lifted his non-shooting arm to steady his shot, Joe hit him in the back with five rounds from one of the Glock semi-automatic pistols. The three figures running behind a broken tabletop didn't stop until they'd reached the edge of the clearing. Joe ran toward them. When the three stepped out from behind the improvised shield, he emptied the second Glock into the one not named Morgan.

Chapter Twenty

The fire spread quickly. Tom, Joe, and Luke ran past the burned-out remains of Tom's rental car and Bobby Travis's truck, tucking their noses and mouths inside their shirts to filter the smoke. A crescendo of sirens wailed in the distance. When the three Morgans reached the lake road, Tom leaned over to catch his breath. Pulling his brother aside, he gasped, "Your pal Grogan will be here any minute."

Joe coughed and spat. "So what?"

"So, tell me what you want me to tell him."

"Nothing. Keep your mouth shut."

"For god's sake, Joe, there are two dead bodies back there, spent shells from a running gunfight, a forest fire, a burned-out cabin, a burned-out rental car, a disabled truck, and a child witness. What do you want me to say when the guy who's looking for any possible way to put you behind bars gets here and starts asking questions? What's your plan?"

Joe glared.

Tom stood upright and took a deep breath. "Do you want me to tell the truth? That could get complicated."

"I want you to shut up."

"With a pair of dead bodies back there?"

"Kidnappers' bodies."

Tom shook his head and hauled in another lungful of air. "The guy with the gun, maybe. But the guy in the cabin was clueless. He picked Luke up by the side of the road with a busted bike, left a voicemail with Bonnie, took Luke to where he was staying, fed him, and waited for Bonnie to return his call. He was no kidnapper."

"Bullshit."

"He didn't know about the bonds. His story about Luke's busted bike and calling Bonnie is probably what Luke is going to tell the state troopers when they get here and start asking questions. If that story checks out, you just shot an innocent, unarmed man."

"What about the phone call?" Joe growled. "Luke in exchange for MadDog's retirement stash?"

"I don't think the guy in the cabin knew anything about that."

"Like hell, he didn't. That makes no sense."

"Only because we don't have all the pieces yet. But whatever story we tell better be consistent with what Luke's going to say when Grogan gets here and what comes out later. And it better explain the carnage back there without sending both of us to Auburn: you for murder and me as an accessory. I have a life I'd like to get back to."

Joe scoffed and spat.

Tom looked back toward the burning woods. "Okay. How about this? You got a phone call from some Good Samaritan who said he picked up your kid with a busted bike by the side of the road and that you should come collect them both. But the pickup spot turned out to be an ambush. You don't know who the caller was. You didn't recognize a voice. But this is the second time in a month that you've been ambushed in the woods. This time it was someone with a gun, not a bow and arrow and, luckily, you won the shootout."

Joe looked thoughtful.

"If you think that story has holes in it, now's the time to patch them. But it fits the facts as we know them, and it's consistent with what Luke is likely to say. You can't feed the kid some fairy tale and then expect him to stick to it through a police grilling. Not in his condition. And you don't have a better story ready, or you'd be shoving it down my throat right now."

Joe took his time to answer as the sound of sirens and crackling forest grew louder. "What are you doing here?" he asked quietly.

"I was with you when you got the Good Samaritan call. I came along with you to pick up Luke and his busted bike."

"I mean, what are you doing in Coldwater?"

"Other than trying to help you figure out who killed mom and flushing my career down the toilet?"

"What are you doing here, Tommy?"

Tom hesitated. It was no time to be throwing jabs. But he launched one anyway. "Maybe I'm here to save your family."

"From what?"

"From you."

* * *

The fire trucks arrived first. The fire chief called for additional trucks and aerial assistance from Fort Drum while his men hosed the undergrowth so the fire wouldn't jump the road. Tom had managed to hold onto his phone, and he left a message on Bonnie's to let her know that Luke was okay and that he would be home shortly.

When Grogan and the other trooper arrived, Joe told the story that Tom had outlined. The trooper managed to look both disbelieving and uninterested at the same time. He told Joe to get into the state car.

"No thanks. My brother and I have some unfinished business."

"I'm not offering you a ride," said Grogan. "I'm arresting you for assault."

Joe smirked. "What are you smoking, Grogan? Two lowlifes kidnapped my son and held him in that cabin back there. A Heller cabin, in case you didn't know. That name still mean anything to you?"

"An act of vandalism in the presence of the property owner constitutes assault in this state. Does that still mean anything to you, *Sheriff?* Get in the car."

"Shit for brains, the kidnappers set that fire."

"We'll see about that. Right now, I'm arresting you for assault and false imprisonment, for vandalizing your wife's car in her presence to intimidate her and prevent her from leaving home with her children."

Tom interrupted. "Trooper Grogan, this is the second time in as many weeks that someone has ambushed and tried to kill my brother. You might want to check prints on the bodies back there against what you get off that arrow fragment I gave you."

Grogan looked at Joe and smirked. "There weren't any prints."

Only an act of will kept angry disbelief from Tom's voice. "Then, as we discussed," he said, "if the blood on the arrow fragment is Joe's and there are no prints on the fragment, then the shooting was pre-meditated."

"Or it's deer blood," said Grogan. "We can take a sample from the sheriff when we get back to the station. We'll be testing him for drugs and alcohol, too."

"Kiss my ass," said Joe.

* * *

One of the firemen drove Tom and Luke back to Mary's apartment so that Tom could pick up Herbert Ball's Buick. He did not look forward to explaining to Avis how someone had turned their top-of-the-line luxury car into a two thousand-pound Molotov cocktail. And he didn't hold much hope that the state troopers would issue a report backing his story.

Luke had said nothing since those first few minutes in the cabin. But there were questions that needed to be asked and answered, preferably by a kindly uncle rather than a suspicious state trooper. On the drive home, Tom began by telling his nephew how brave he had been and how proud he was of him. "Morgan men are tough," said Tom. "But someone your age who can keep his wits under gunfire is someone to be reckoned with, now and in the future."

Luke started to smile, but then he looked away.

Tom continued. "Helping your dad get to the hospital the day he got shot with an arrow couldn't have been easy, either."

Luke's shoulders rounded, and he continued to stare out the car window.

"Did you see anyone else in the woods that day besides you and your dad?"

Luke nodded and leaned his head against the glass.

"Did you see your dad get shot?"

Luke moved his head from side to side.

Tom reached over and rubbed his nephew's head. "You're one tough hombre, Mister Morgan."

Luke stood stiffly while his mother hugged and fussed over him. The girls remained seated on the living room couch. Both looked tired. "Hi, Uncle Tom," said Meghan. Her sister gave a weak smile and waived a thin hand. Tom spoke to Luke. "I need to talk to your mom. You should go change your clothes."

Bonnie gave Tom a wry look. "You could use a change, too. And a bath. You smell like smoke. Do you want to do that first? I can give you something of Joe's."

"Maybe later. Your boy's been through an ordeal in the last few hours. I need to fill you in."

Bonnie led the way to the back porch, stopping to pour a lemonade for Tom and to add something to hers. Sitting in the Adirondack chairs, facing the lake and the setting sun, she spoke first. "I'm sure you've both had an adventure, and I want to know exactly where my husband has had my son for the last six hours. But Joe is in jail, right? Just tell me that part's true. The state trooper said the protective order came through."

"He's in jail. Although for how long, I don't know."

She looked thoughtful. "Then we still need to get out of here."

And Luke needs to stay put.

"Your son has just been through something scary, Bonnie, on top of having witnessed his father get shot through the back with an arrow. A road trip to nowhere may not be the best thing right now."

Bonnie opened her mouth as if to retort and as if she hadn't heard the word 'scary'. But instead, she looked away.

Just tell her.

"Where were you thinking of taking them?" He knew he was stalling.

"I have a friend..."

"Is she in Coldwater?"

Bonnie grimaced. "Him." Then, catching Tom's look, she added, "It's not like that." She explained about her old high school admirer: loyal, undemanding and reliable. "He's a nice man. But it's complicated."

"Three kids and a violent ex? I'd say so."

"Well, it hasn't deterred him, thank God."

Tom felt the moment slipping away.

"But I'm not looking to add a new man to my life, at least not right now. I won't be a user."

Tom wrapped his hand around the cold glass and let her talk.

"But Joe is out of control. And he's gotten more violent. That's the most important thing in all this. That's why we can't stay. Why I can't stay."

"Bonnie, if it's money…"

She took a long swallow of her drink. "Money is a factor. I won't deny that. But I won't sell myself to put a roof over my children's heads. Or set that example for my girls. Or Luke." She lapsed into silence. After a moment, she asked, "Can't a man just be a friend?"

Tom compressed his lips. "If you're thinking about a twenty-year commitment to help raise a family…I'd have to say no."

Her face sagged.

Quit stalling, Tommy. Just tell her. Your son was kidnapped, and his father shot one of the kidnappers right in front of him. You can't toss the boy into the back of the family jalopy and skip town. He's going to need help. Possibly for a long time.

"Where is this friend now?" he asked, still stalling.

"I don't know. I called him right after I called you, after Luke ran off and Joe yanked the wires out of my car. Mark was going to look for Luke, but I guess Luke met up with his father. I haven't heard from him since that one phone call."

Tom felt a tingling at the back of his neck. The question came out almost as a whisper. "Can I ask Mark's last name?"

Bonnie looked wary. "Why?"

"Is it Tremblay?"

"Yes. What's going on?"

Shit.

In a stilted monotone, Tom told Bonnie the same story that he and Joe had told the state troopers. "I'm sorry," he said when he'd finished. There was nothing else to say.

At some point during his recitation, Bonnie slumped back in her chair and closed her eyes. Though her mouth remained open while she hauled in shallow breaths. After Tom finished, she opened her eyes and sat upright. "I don't believe it," she said. "You're telling me that my son was trapped in a burning cabin? And that my husband killed two people right in front of him?"

"Yes. And I think Luke may also have seen who shot his dad with an arrow. That it may have been one of the kidnappers."

"Dear God."

"He's going to need help, Bonnie. Moving him back to Canada or anywhere else right now can't be a good idea."

Bonnie stood and paced. "And Joe shot Mark?"

"Yes, but that's not..."

"That son-of-a bitch."

"Bonnie, he was confronting two men who were holding Luke for ransom, one of whom set fire to the cabin with Luke and me in it and who was shooting at all of us."

Bonnie shook her head in denial. When she spoke, her voice trembled. "I don't believe it. Mark would not have taken Luke to some cabin in the woods. He would have brought him here. If I wasn't home and Mark couldn't get me on the phone, he'd have waited. He would never have called Joe."

"I don't think he did. I think his cousin did, somebody named Travis."

Bonnie pulled in her chin. "Travis?"

"That's what Tremblay said, yes."

Bonnie stood, turned, and strode purposefully into the house. Should he follow her? He twirled his empty glass and stared at the prism of fading sunlight wrapped around its surface. Follow her and say what? I'm sorry your husband shot your hapless admirer. Or more to the point, this isn't about your wannabe boyfriend, Bonnie. Or your cheating husband. It's about your *son.*

When she returned, she handed Tom a folded sheet of colored paper. "I didn't keep the envelope. But it was postmarked yesterday from Coldwater. A woman's handwriting. No signature."

Dear Mrs. Morgan,

I hesitate to write to you. But you're well-liked in this town. And some, including myself, are uncomfortable knowing what you may not, and which you certainly have the right to know. Your husband, our sheriff, remains a frequent visitor to a well-known lovers' lane just outside of town. He's been seen there often in the company of a Mrs. Crystal Travis. What went on in Mrs. Travis's parked car this last Thursday afternoon is anyone's guess. But you have three lovely children, and those who care about you and them don't like to see you humiliated."

Tom scrutinized the letter, the paper, and the handwriting. "Have there been other notes like this?"

"Two before I left with the kids last year. This is the first since we've been back."

"All from the same person?"

"It's the same paper and handwriting."

Tom looked at the letter again. "Do you mind if I keep this?"

She waved her hand dismissively. "I don't care. But you have to understand, Tom, I can't be here when Joe gets out. It's not safe. I have to leave. And the kids have to come with me. All of them."

Tom stood. "What if Joe doesn't get bail? Or at least not any time soon?"

"Can you make that happen?"

"I think so. In the meantime, keep Luke here, okay? The boy needs Mom and chicken soup more than anything else. And if some state trooper comes around to talk to him, bolt the door. Paulie Grogan is after my brother's hide. If he gets his hands on Luke, he won't hesitate to use him to get what he wants. The consequences to the kid be damned."

Chapter Twenty-One

Tom left Bonnie and drove to Town Hall. On the way, he tried to put order to his scattered thoughts: Luke needs help. So does Bonnie. Who killed Mom and Herbert Ball? Why did Joe shoot an unarmed Tremblay? Paint samples. Europe…? He pulled the car to the side of the road and stared at the lake, hoping to slow his mind. It didn't help. What was he going to say to Joe? Your kid's a mess. You're a mess. Paulie Grogan's a slime ball idiot, but he's lying in the weeds waiting for you. He's got resources, and he's not going away. You shot an unarmed, innocent man. Your wife's going to leave you. You're dangerous.

The last was key. The rest might be fixed. But the hard truth was that Joe had become dangerous. It may not have been his nature to begin with. But over time, little brother had made himself into something scary. Always physical, now he was violent. He used to have rules. Now, he didn't. Left to continue, that would surely lead to tragedy.

In the basement of Town Hall, Tom found Trooper Grogan sitting behind MadDog's old desk, holding a piece of burnt paper in a pair of outsized tweezers. A charred leather satchel took up most of the desktop. "Know what this is?" the trooper asked with an apparent effort to suppress his usual sarcasm.

"No," said Tom, momentarily surprised that Grogan was doing what looked like real police work.

"It's got the word 'bank' on it." Grogan dropped the paper into a plastic baggie and then patted the charred bag. "There's a few more scraps like it inside this. Which is all that's left of that cabin you two torched."

"One of the kidnappers torched it. With me and my nephew inside."

"So you say. I've got questions about that, too."

"I'm here to see my brother."

Grogan motioned to the chair next to the desk. "First things first." He turned the computer screen to face the visitor chair, clicked its mouse, and watched two lines appear on the screen. The first was a series of letters and numerals: CH93 0076 2011 6238 5295 7, and the other was a series of numerals: 1875325. "Does any of that mean anything to you?" he asked.

"Specifically? No."

"How about 'generally'?"

The numbers were familiar enough for someone in Tom's world. But what was Paulie Grogan doing with an account code for a Swiss private bank? And what was it doing on Joe's computer?

"Morgan?"

Tom folded his hands. "The longer line is in the format of a numbered Swiss bank account. A two-letter country code, two-digit check number, five-character bank code, and a twelve-digit account number. The shorter, all-digit entry might be an account balance. But I'm guessing you already know all that."

"Impressive," said Grogan, his voice a mocking compliment. "How is it that you recognize a Swiss bank account number?"

"I have an international legal practice, Trooper Grogan. Some of my clients reside in countries where Swiss bank accounts are lawful. How is it that you know about them?"

Grogan ignored the question and continued with the demo he'd obviously been working on. "The BCI forensic computer group cracked the passcodes to your brother's office computer. In addition to an illegal Swiss bank account, they found this." Grogan clicked the mouse and watched a grainy black-and-white photo of a grotesquely mutilated male body fill the screen. "There's a video, too, showing how the man in that picture got that way. It's called a 'snuff movie, or so I'm told.'"

Tom clamped his teeth. *Jesus Christ, Joe.*

"You look upset, Morgan. You didn't know that your brother had a Swiss bank account? Or is it his taste in movies that disturbs you?"

Tom looked away. When he regained a semblance of mental balance and found his tongue, he asked. "Is there a date on those files? When they were created, and when they were last visited?"

Grogan turned the screen around and smiled. "I can't say."

"But you are saying that they belong to my brother."

"They're on his computer."

Tom thought out loud. "He could have been investigating something. It could be research. Depending on the file dates, they could even pre-date his tenure as sheriff. On its own, none of that is illegal, Trooper Grogan. Disturbing, perhaps. But not illegal."

Grogan shook his head. "Save it for the prosecutor, mister lawyer, if your brother really wants to go that route: prison, scandal, wife's and kiddo's faces plastered across the front page of the Gazette." The trooper's smile was a creepy mix of low-caste predator and lower reptile. "A man who loved his family might want to avoid all that."

Tom waited. Everyone had their preferred style of negotiation. Grogan was about to reveal his. Tom guessed that it would be squeeze, quid pro quo or a combination of both. There was no chance of it being win/win. "I'm listening," he prompted.

"Good. You're going to tell your brother what you just saw here and that BCI forensics is coming up with more. He'll know what that means."

Tom waited.

"And then you're going to tell him that if he claims he was chasing poachers when he got shot with that arrow, we'll let him put in for retirement."

"Put in? That's not the same as getting."

"It's been arranged, counselor. Don't worry."

"Anything else?"

"Yes. Tell him the Black River trooper barracks is taking over here as of now, whether he files for retirement or not. Coldwater won't be needing a one-man sheriff's department after this. Certainly not one that's into snuff movies and Swiss bank accounts." Grogan paused for effect. "If that should ever get out."

Tom made a mental note. *The squeeze.*

* * *

Grogan escorted Tom back to the cells where Joe and Tom had played as little boys. And where later, when Tom needed a quiet place to cram for school exams, he had spent many a quiet hour alone.

"You've got a visitor, Morgan."

Joe lay on a plywood bunk, hands clasped behind his head, staring at the ceiling. "I haven't decided yet, Grogan, whether to flay you alive or just take you out to the middle of Coldwater Lake and keel haul you. You got a preference?"

"Threatening a law enforcement officer, now?"

"It's not a threat, punk. I'm going to do it."

Speaking to Tom, Grogan said, "You've got twenty minutes."

When the trooper left, Tom took a plastic chair from beneath the dust-caked window and brought it next to the cell bars that were the only things likely preventing his brother from carrying out his threat. "Bonnie and the girls are okay," said Tom. "Thanks for asking. Grogan wants you to retire on disability."

"Paulie Grogan can eat shit and die."

Tom continued in the same chit-chat tone. "He asked me to tell you that the BCI ran your computer through their password-cracking software and he showed me some of what they found. He says there's more."

Joe continued to stare at the ceiling.

"A Swiss bank account and some snuff movies, to start with."

Joe yawned. "Are you Grogan's messenger boy now?"

Tom dropped the chit-chat tone, and his voice became serious as well as puzzled. "I can't cover a Swiss bank account, Joe. And your taste in movies is...disturbing."

Joe yawned. "It's MadDog's account, Tommy. And they're his movies."

Tom was taken aback, but only briefly. "They're on *your* computer, Joe."

Joe rolled over on the cot and sat up. "I don't owe you an explanation,

Tommy. Or anyone else."

"Is that what you're going to tell the prosecutors? Mind your own business?"

Joe swung his feet to the floor and sat on the edge of the cot, lifting his chin in the air as if considering a distasteful sharing of confidence. He glared at Tom. "Fine. You remember Pop passed away kind of sudden like?" It was a rhetorical question that did not require a response, and Joe didn't wait for one. "Well, he didn't leave behind a helpful list of passwords and account numbers. At least Mom didn't find anything in the house, and I didn't find anything in the office. But the files on his computer that weren't password protected had everything the department needed. So, I figured the rest were personal. Guess I was right."

"So, what are they doing on your computer?"

Joe took a moment to answer, or more likely to decide whether he was going to. Eventually, he just shrugged and said, "The office upgraded to new computers about six years ago. The guys who did the setup copied everything off the old computer, protected and unprotected, and downloaded them onto the new one. They said we could send the protected files to someplace that had password-cracking software, but it would cost a couple of grand. We didn't have a couple of extra grand in the budget then, so we didn't do it. Grogan was there then. He knows that."

Tom took a moment to reflect. It was a good story: internally consistent, difficult to check or refute. Parts of it might even be true. But if the state forensic IT people could determine when the files were last accessed before being cracked, and it proved to be some time in the last six years, then the story wouldn't hold. Had Joe thought of that?

Not wanting to go down that rabbit hole, he asked the question he'd come to ask before Grogan sidetracked him with the spoils of his computer dumpster diving. There was no point putting it off. "Why did you shoot the guy who ran out of the cabin with me and Luke."

Joe cracked his knuckles and stared at Tom. He didn't answer.

"He hadn't hurt Luke," Tom prompted. "He didn't know about the ransom, and he wasn't armed."

"He was a Heller for chrissakes! Who do you think killed MadDog?"

"So, you're going to kill all the Hellers? Is that the plan now? Or just a selected few?"

"Don't be a damned Boy Scout, Tommy."

"You told me once that your law enforcement philosophy was to lock up the dangerous and let God take care of the guilty. That the Hellers and the other local bad boys were like weeds in your garden. That you plucked up the violent and ambitious and left the others alone if they didn't get out of hand. It was a question of resources, you said. One cop could only do so much."

"That's right."

"So, what happened to 'live and let live, as long as no one got out of hand'?"

"They got out of hand."

"Tremblay? That man was harmless!"

"The Hellers, Tommy. One of them slit Dad's throat, in case you've forgotten, shot me in the back, and murdered Mom and her boyfriend. Do you really expect me to sit around and do nothing?"

"You don't know that a Heller did any of those things, Joe. Or are you planning to kill them all, just in case? How about actual guilt? And proof? And due process?"

"Listen to me, brother. If someone kills our mother, kidnaps my kid, or tries to kill me, they are not going to die of old age. Do you seriously have a problem with that?"

"What I've got a problem with, Joe, is you appointing yourself judge, jury, and executioner without a shred of remorse for having shot an unarmed, innocent man."

"He was a Heller, Tommy. He kidnapped my son."

Chapter Twenty-Two

"My brother is thinking it over."

Grogan sneered. "What's there to think about? If he doesn't take the deal, I give the prosecutors everything our IT people found on his computer."

"He's not used to being squeezed."

"Too bad. Frankly, I hope he does say no. Some people would like him to go without a fuss. But I'd be happy to put him in Auburn."

"You don't like my brother."

"I don't like your whole family, Morgan. You've had a lock on the Coldwater sheriff's office for as long as anyone can remember. But Morgans have never upheld the law; they just spit on it. And anyone who works with them gets tarred with the same brush."

"Is that why you left?"

"That's right. I just couldn't stand the stink anymore."

* * *

Tom left Grogan muttering recriminations under his breath. He wasn't wrong. But even if everything fell his way, Grogan didn't have what was needed to put Joe away for any meaningful length of time. The trooper might not even be able to put him away at all. Bonnie could refuse to testify. If she did, a misdemeanor conviction wouldn't necessarily end the career of a popular sheriff. If Grogan couldn't disprove Joe's assertion that the Swiss bank account and other password-protected files on the department computer predated his time as sheriff, then the trooper had nothing.

Tom got into Herbert's Buick and drove up the lake road, sunk in weary debate with his conscience. As the 19th century English politician, Lord Acton, had once famously declared: power corrupts, and absolute power corrupts absolutely. Joe's power in Coldwater was not absolute. But he had clearly come to believe that he could get away with almost anything, from intimidating his wife to shooting an unarmed innocent man. Equally clear was that if, in his sole and final judgment, someone deserved to die, then he, Joe, would make that happen. More than the authoritarian shibboleth of "the end justifies the means," the Coldwater sheriff had apparently appointed himself judge, jury, and executioner in all matters pertaining to Morgan "family business." The niceties of proof and due process be damned.

As Tom drove past turn-of-the-century houses with their well-manicured lawns and wide wrap-around porches, he struggled with the growing conviction that his brother could not be allowed to walk free as long as he wore a badge and carried a gun. Paulie Grogan did not have what was necessary to make that happen. But did Tom? And if he used it, what would become of the Morgan family then? Or what remained of it.

Tom parked Herbert's car in front of the church rectory, knocked at the side door, and waited for the housekeeper, Mrs. Flynn, to appear and escort him to Fr. Gauss's study. When Tom entered the room, the priest stepped from behind his trestle table desk and came forward to give him a gentle hug. "Glad to see you in one piece," he said. "Jack Thompson called to ask me if I knew anything about the Morgan brothers being involved in a gun battle. I told him no."

"Joe was involved. I just watched."

"Dear God. Do you want to talk about it?"

Tom stared through the lake-side windows at white-capped waves rolling past the weather-beaten church dock. "I don't know the whole story, Father. And the part I do know might put you in a compromising position if I shared it."

Gauss returned to his seat and gestured for Tom to take one of the straight-backed chairs. "Then how can I help?"

"Let me think out loud for a minute. Then, if you have advice or want to tell me that I'm off my rocker, please do it."

Tom spoke for twenty minutes and then sat back in his chair and waited. It was a lot to lay on a priest, even one as smart and as worldly as Father Gauss. Tom wasn't sure that unburdening his soul to his old friend had been kind or even wise. But it was done. Now, he waited.

"That's quite a scheme, Tommy. And a profound responsibility if you go ahead with it."

"I know, Father. But doing nothing feels like watching a train wreck from a safe distance while innocent bystanders are left to fend for themselves."

"Yes. But if you go through with what you just outlined, you can't just leave on the next plane. Or any time in the foreseeable future."

Tom looked up at the ceiling.

"Do you remember the sign that Mrs. Oliver used to have in her newspaper store," Gauss asked. "'*You break it, you bought it?*'"

"I remember."

Gauss leaned across the desk. "What you propose won't just clip your brother's wings. It will clip yours, too. Or it should. Perhaps permanently."

Tom took a deep breath. "And what about the so-called 'good' brother adopting the methods of 'ethically challenged' brother: lock up the dangerous and let God take care of the guilty? Got any thoughts on that bit of irony?"

"Are you asking me if I believe that the end justifies the means?"

"Does it? Ever?"

Gauss took a moment to respond. "To be honest, I don't know how I come down on that one. I'm reminded, though, that when Christ threw the moneylenders out of the temple, he didn't ask them politely. He just kicked some Pharasitic butt. Quite the opposite of his usual 'turn the other cheek' preaching. But the choice you've created for yourself is familiar enough: make the best decision in a complex situation where there may be no good choices. Or walk away and do nothing. You're a good man, Thomas. Think carefully about this. Then, trust your judgment. I do."

* * *

"My brother says, 'No deal.'"

Grogan looked pissed, but not surprised. "Fine. I've got him on assault: terrorizing his wife, putting a guy in the hospital and later killing him. I've also got a Swiss bank account and a bunch of snuff movies."

"That's not…"

Grogan held up his hand. "Plus a call from a witness who says he saw a truck hit your brother's Silverado, with your mother and her boyfriend inside, just before it flipped over and killed them. The witness got a partial license plate." Grogan did a drum roll with his hands on the top of Joe's desk. And it matches…"

Tom waited.

"The plate on a truck belonging to one Robert Travis of 8 Bullet Hole Rd, Coldwater, NY. Husband of Crystal Travis of the same address, who…" Grogan repeated the drum roll, "has been screwing the Coldwater sheriff… and whose husband's truck is currently a burned-out wreck at the site of a shoot-out between said sheriff and the now deceased Mr. Travis."

Tom felt the corners of his mouth tighten. "And you think that means?"

"That the so-called "ambush" that you and your brother described was a trap set by your brother to get rid of the husband of the woman he was screwing."

Tom rolled his eyes.

"Were you there," Grogan demanded, "when he supposedly got a phone call, allegedly from Travis, about coming to pick up your nephew? How do you know your brother didn't call Travis and set *him* up?"

Tom shook his head. "I'm not sure I can count all the holes in that theory, Trooper Grogan. Starting with its failure to account for that guy Tremblay holding Joe's son hostage in a Heller cabin."

"We didn't find any weapons there."

"A full-grown man does not need a weapon to hold a kid who won't be shaving for another five years." Then, returning to Grogan's story of an eyewitness to the crash that killed Mary Morgan and her boyfriend, he asked, "When did this call come in? And who took it?"

"This morning. I took it."

"And when is this witness coming in to give a statement?"

Grogan didn't answer.

Tom scoffed. "Seriously? You think you can bluff my brother with a fairy tale like that?"

Grogan lifted a hand and pointed toward the door. "Your brother's going to jail, Morgan. That's no bluff."

"For misdemeanor assault, maybe. And then what? You said that your computer gurus recovered more from Joe's computer than what you showed me. Where is it? What is it?"

"We're done talking, Morgan."

"For chrissakes, Grogan. That was a bluff, too?"

"I've got what I need to put your brother behind bars. I don't need anymore."

"For six months. Assuming his wife testifies, and the DA gets a conviction. Then what? Your worst nightmare comes back, bigger and badder than ever, runs for re-election, and wins in a landslide. Then his first order of business will be to come after *you*."

"I can take care of myself."

Is this what I have to work with?

Tom almost abandoned his plan right there. But he could not ignore Joe's killing of the innocent Tremblay and his complete lack of remorse for it. He did not want his brother to spend the rest of his life in prison for killing an accidental kidnapper in a parental rage. But his brother's license to bully and kill had to come to an end. Permanently. *And what about Grogan...?*

"Morgan, you're spacing."

Tom tried to suppress the sneer that fought to take permanent hold of his face. In as calm a voice as he could summon, he asked, "Suppose you had something that would put my brother away for longer than one election cycle? Long enough to put your own guy in charge and fold the Coldwater sheriff's department into the state troopers like your bosses have wanted to forever?"

Grogan's face was bland and disbelieving. "You've got something like that?"

"Let's say I do."

"And you'd give it to me? On your own brother?"

Tom's face hardened. "My brother is a dangerous bully. The latest in a long line of them, as you've pointed out. But I don't want him to end up dead like our father. I'd also like to see the next generation of Morgans have a chance to be something other than badasses with a badge. But I don't see them abandoning the family franchise as long as their father remains a larger-than-life Superman. Someone who can do what he wants to whoever he wants whenever he wants to."

Grogan held Tom's gaze.

"I don't hate my brother, Trooper Grogan. But we both know he has to be stopped."

Grogan nodded slowly. "So, what have you got for me?"

"For starters, a crash course on Swiss bank accounts. Just for you. No other law enforcement involved. If you pass, I'll give you the rest."

"I don't like games, Morgan. Why should I trust you, or you trust me?"

"You shouldn't, and I don't." Tom struggled to keep the anger and loathing out of his voice. "But remember when I told you that there was a second piece of arrow likely stuck in a tree near where I found the first fragment?"

"Yeah."

"When I went back there after I told you about it, I found two sets of boot prints around the tree it used to be stuck in. One set was mine, of course. I believe you know who the other belongs to."

"It's my job to look for evidence."

"And I've got it. A fixed, three-bladed, one-inch broadhead, carbon fiber shaft, dried blood and, I'm willing to bet, prints. All of them are in a safe place now. But if something were to happen to my brother while he's in jail, or if he doesn't get out when we agreed, or if I start hearing rumors about snuff movies or anything else, I'll have all those pieces tested. Then, if there *are* prints... Well, we know whose those will be. Don't we?"

Grogan glared but said nothing.

"You shot my brother in the back, you sanctimonious coward. Couldn't stand the stink?"

Grogan started to protest, but Tom held up his hand.

"We can go down that path if you like: Joe for misdemeanor assault and you for attempted murder. Or we can make a deal."

Grogan glared but remained silent.

"You're going to arrange a state-paid vacation for my brother. Say, two to three years, someplace safe where he can figure out what he wants to do with the rest of his life. You make that happen, and that arrow fragment with the blood and the prints remains where it is—in a safe place, untested."

Grogan seethed.

"But if you don't do that, or if something unfortunate happens to my brother, now or later," Tom leaned forward and placed his palms on MadDog's desk, "Then I'll get that arrow fragment tested and give the results to Jack Thompson at the Gazette. Or, if he's still alive, to Joe. And God help you then."

* * *

Tom left Grogan to simmer in whatever unsavory brine of frustration and fear his tiny little mind now foundered in, and went back to the cells to have a word with Joe. Stretched on top of a foam-covered plank bed, his face turned toward the ceiling, the soon-to-be former Coldwater sheriff lay motionless where Tom had left him earlier.

"I told you to get lost," Joe growled.

Tom pulled the plastic visitor's chair up to the bars. "Luke sends his love. Nice of you to ask. Bonnie's mostly recovered from your latest chest-beating display. The girls… they're a little tense."

"What are you doing here?"

"We need to rehearse. You're going to plead guilty to a Class E felony—shooting an unarmed Mark Tremblay. You'll get three to five and be out in two."

"I told you no deal."

"And I told Trooper Grogan that if you don't change your mind, I'll give him what he needs to put you away for twenty to thirty. The bearer bonds, the Swiss bank account, the fact that Tremblay was unarmed and had his hands up when you shot him."

"Bullshit on the hands."

"So you say. But if you're going to look a gift horse in the mouth, I'm going to say different."

Joe's eyes were slits. "Why are you doing this?"

"Because you're my little brother, and I feel responsible for you."

Joe scoffed.

"Do you remember when MadDog used to make fun of my teeth?" Tom asked.

"Yeah, he used to say that you looked like a horse eating an apple through a fence. So what?"

"Or that I threatened to bury an ax in his skull the last time he said it?"

"I'll bet he wet his pants."

"Sadly not. So I went to Montreal, got my teeth fixed, acquired a French girlfriend and an interest in exchange rates that helped me make the pile I used to get out of here."

"You're boring me, bright boy. You got a point?"

"Just this. Going head-to-head with our bully father made me learn something that *you* need to learn now, too. An opponent who can't beat you on your terms, can still beat you on theirs if they're persistent and lucky. You never learned that, because you've never had to fight on anyone else's terms. But that's what Grogan and the Hellers are trying to do to you now. You're tougher than any Heller and smarter than Paulie Grogan. But they've got time and numbers on their side. Frankie Heller is dead, and so is Bobby Travis. But the Hellers are happy to wait in the weeds until one of them finally gets you. Paulie Grogan will keep using the resources of the state troopers to create a set-up that, sooner or later, will stick. Then it will be thirty to life, not three to five and out in two. If they all keep at it, sooner or later, one of them will get you."

Joe glared.

"I'm saving your ass with this deal, Joe."

"Why?"

"Because like I said, you're my little brother and I feel responsible for you."

"Well, big brother. Like I said, no deal."

"It's not a deal, Joe. It's what's going to happen. I'm explaining it to you. I'm not asking."

Joe remained silent. When he finally spoke, it was in a curt, menacing growl. "This isn't over, Tommy."

"Yes, it is, brother. All of it."

Chapter Twenty-Three

Tom left Joe stewing in a dark brew of anger, frustration, and resentment and then drove down Route 6 to the office of the Coldwater Gazette. Tom and the newspaper's owner, Jack Thompson, had met several years ago when Tom was helping Joe investigate the murder of Billy Pearce, the younger brother of a woman with whom both Tom and Joe each had a relationship. When the national media erroneously reported the Pearce murder as a "terrorist plot foiled," Tom gave Thompson the real story on the condition that he not publish it until Tom had time to insulate himself from the fallout. When the Gazette finally published, portraying half a dozen government agencies as little more than lying Keystone Cops, the paper won a Pulitzer. Tom and the newspaper's owner had done a few favors for each other after that. They were not friends, but the relationship was cordial and sometimes beneficial.

Leaving the Buick at the far end of the parking lot, Tom climbed the back stairs to the newspaper's second-floor offices and approached the long white drafting table that served as the newspaperman's command post. "Rumor has it you're looking for me," he said.

Thompson looked up from his computer and turned in his chair. "My sources tell me that an ambulance brought two bullet-ridden corpses to the Coldwater Hospital morgue yesterday afternoon. That the bodies were taken from the site of a gun battle featuring the Morgan brothers and a burned-out cabin. They tell me that the Coldwater sheriff was hauled away in handcuffs by the state troopers and that his brother, who was with him, is on the lam." He picked up a pen and spiral notepad. "Care to comment?"

"I don't like lamb."

"Comment, wise guy. Or I go to press with what I've got: the multi-generational Morgan family scandal that the whole town's been waiting years to see in print."

"What scandal is that, Jack?"

"Corrupt, violent cops who do as they please, the law be damned. Sons who follow in their father's bloody footsteps like some rogue cop dynasty."

"You've been waiting a long time to print that story."

Thompson's face remained impassive; his pen poised over his reporter's notepad.

"You might get to write it one of these days. But not today."

Thompson scoffed. "Why not? I've got a file as thick as the Manhattan Yellow Pages on the murderous Morgan clan. It goes back decades."

"Because yesterday's rumors don't sell today's papers. But I can give you the real story of what happened to those two corpses: who did what to whom and why. If you're interested. It's a hell of a story. The kind that might get the Gazette another Pulitzer."

Thompson leaned back in his chair and folded his arms across his chest. "I'm listening."

Tom dropped a plastic bag sealed with duct tape onto the newspaperman's desk. "Inside that bag is a piece of blood-covered arrow shaft. The blood belongs to my brother, and the fingerprints on it, if any, belong to the person who shot him through the back with that arrow."

"And who might that be?"

"A member of a competing law enforcement agency."

Thompson whistled. "And you can prove that?"

"Forensics can prove it. The blood on the arrow fragment is Joe's, and the prints, if any, belong to whoever shot him. But you need me for chain of custody—where and when the arrow fragment was found, by who, and so forth. Otherwise, it's not proof of anything."

"Are you in a position to provide that chain of custody?"

"I am."

Tom explained that the Coldwater sheriff would be spending some time behind bars and that the story used to keep him there would be bogus. "But when he gets out, I'll give you the real story, as well as the chain of custody to prove it. Then you can print the sanguinary history of the Morgan clan, if you want. My brother won't be putting on a uniform again, and neither will any other Morgan."

Thompson looked him up and down. "What's to prevent me from taking this arrow fragment to a lab right now?"

"Nothing. But Joe could have had a nosebleed. Then, some prankster could have rolled an arrow shaft in it and got a patsy to touch it. Criminal Law 101, Jack: Physical evidence is useless without a chain of custody."

"I don't like my paper being used, Morgan."

"Not even for a Pulitzer?"

"Not even."

Tom picked up the plastic bag and stepped away from the table. "I'm sorry, Jack. This has to be take it or leave it. Hold publication until Joe is out of jail, and you can have an exclusive. Otherwise, it goes to the Times."

Thompson glared. "What about those two corpses?"

"I'll wait to hear from you."

* * *

Tom left the Gazette offices and drove back toward town. Jack Thompson could be a prickly curmudgeon. But he would not print a Morgan family exposé based on a file full of rumor and innuendo. That was a bluff. So was the canard that he would willingly pass up a chance for another Pulitzer. Tom was confident that ambition for his small-town paper would be the determining factor in the newspaperman's final decision. He just hoped that Thompson didn't take too long to make up his mind.

Leaving Herbert Ball's car on the street in front of the Coldwater Bank, Tom went inside to confront Andrew Ryan. When the receptionist apologized that Mr. Ryan was not in the office, Tom pulled the end of his nose *à la* Pinocchio and took the carpeted steps to Ryan's corner office two at a time. The banker was talking into the intercom when Tom appeared at his door. "He's here," said Ryan. "No. No need to call the police."

Ryan gestured toward the chair in front of his desk. He looked tired and his skin had the color of three-day-old fish. "Do I need a lawyer," he asked quietly.

Tom ignored the question and laid a manila folder on top of Ryan's desk. Then he pushed it toward the banker. "I think this is what you were looking for."

"I didn't know I was looking for anything."

"Open it."

The banker picked up a pair of wire-rimmed reading glasses and flipped through the folder's contents. "Where did you get this?"

"In the trunk of a car belonging to the deceased Herbert Bell Shea."

"I see."

"Do you?"

Ryan turned to stare out the window. "It might be better if you explain. I don't want to presume."

Tom leaned toward the banker. "The last time I was here, you said that you weren't sure if Herbert Ball or Herbert Ball Shea was a shareholder in Coldwater Bank. That was a lie."

Ryan continued to look out the window.

"According to the board minutes in that file, Herbert Ball Shea was, in fact, the majority shareholder in Coldwater Bank."

Andrew remained silent.

"That he had the right to redeem his shares at a pre-set price well in excess of the bank's current value. And that he had given notice of his intent to exercise that right unless the other shareholders—principally yourself—agreed to surrender a significant portion of their shares to him."

Ryan turned to face him. "And from that, you conclude?"

"That Herbert Ball was squeezing you. That had he gone through with the exercise of his redemption rights, the other shareholders—again, principally you—would be left with almost nothing."

"That's business, Tom. It can be unpleasant at times. But unpleasant is not *criminal.*"

"No. But it put you in a rough place. Highly compensated careers like yours don't have a lot of runway left at your age. That had to be maddening, given how you and Shea acquired the capital to form Coldwater Bank in the first place."

Ryan turned again to stare out the window.

"But you got lucky. I haven't seen the bank's shareholder agreement. But if it reads like most, individual shareholdings revert to the corporate treasury at appraised value upon the death of a shareholder."

Ryan's breath was shallow and audible, but he continued to say nothing.

"The timely demise of Herbert Ball Shea saved you from the poor house, didn't it, Andrew? If your bank carries key man insurance, as most do, you'll soon own practically the whole thing. Rags to riches on account of one well-timed accident."

Ryan swiveled his chair away from the window and faced his accuser. "You have a suspicious mind, Tom."

"What I have is motive. Also, multiple streaks of blue paint on the back of what remains of my brother's truck that was rammed from behind and run off the road, killing Herbert Ball Shea and my mother. Impact streaks that happen to be the same shade of blue as a slightly crumpled Mercedes currently parked at the bottom of your driveway."

Ryan shook his head, as if in sadness. "My mother had a minor car accident, as I told you. If either she or I had done what you imply, one of us would surely have had the car repaired by now."

"Unless you realized that any local repair shop would almost certainly notify my brother."

Ryan stood. "You have a creative imagination, Tom. But that's all you have."

"You didn't break into Herbert Shea's apartment looking for that folder, or trash my mother's apartment when you couldn't find it?"

Ryan laughed out loud.

"You left your eyeglasses," said Tom, pointing to the wire-rimmed readers on Ryan's desk. "My brother saw them there the day before the funeral."

"Now you're making things up. I've never been in your mother's apartment.

And there's no reason to believe that I might have a key to it or her boyfriend's apartment."

Tom felt suddenly unsure. His mother's apartment had been trashed, but it had not been broken into. *Whoever entered both Mary's and Herbert's apartments had to have had a key.* He nodded and stood.

"Is that all?" asked Andrew.

"For now. I have a few more questions for your mother."

"She's in Florida. I gave you her number."

"You also told me that Herbert Ball Shea wasn't a shareholder in your bank. You're a poor liar, Andrew."

The banker looked away.

"Call her and tell her that Tommy Morgan is on his way and that he's not going to leave without answers."

"She doesn't want to talk to you."

"I don't blame her."

* * *

Tom eased the Buick down the Ryans' nearly vertical driveway and parked it next to the lakeside house near the kitchen entrance. He carried a small knapsack to the side door, knocked and stood waiting. After a minute or so and several additional knocks, it was obvious that his old teacher had no intention of facing her former pupil again. Rather than do a Joe and kick in the door, Tom returned to the Buick, rolled down the house-side windows, tuned the radio to a popular Quebec rap station, and cranked the volume up to permanent brain damage.

A figure in a faded housecoat appeared at an upstairs window. Tom waved and returned to the kitchen door, rapping again on the painted wood. After another minute or so, the door opened, and the woman behind it grumbled, "You made your point, Thomas. Now turn that noise off before the neighbors think I've lost my mind."

After doing as his old teacher requested, Tom returned and followed her to the sun porch at the back of the house. This time Rosemary Ryan sat down, but she did not wait for him to speak. "All I can say, Thomas Morgan, is that you've got nerve."

Tom looked through the long row of rippled glass at the wind-blown whitecaps undulating across Wilson Cove. *There's no easy way to do this. Just start.*

"My brother was shot through the back with a hunting arrow by a person or persons unknown. His son was kidnapped, and the three of us were shot at by the Heller who orchestrated the kidnapping. My mother and your son's business partner were killed by a hit-and-run driver, identity yet unknown, and afterward their apartments were sacked and searched. That's a lot of lethal violence directed toward the Morgan family in a short period of time. It raises a few questions. Some may be insensitive. But since they can best, and perhaps only, be answered by you and/or your son, I do not intend to leave without answers."

Rosemary Ryan stiffened, and she spoke sharply. "I'm sorry for your family's troubles, Thomas. But I won't be talked to in that tone. And I won't be bullied."

Ignoring her bluster, Tom opened the knapsack that he had carried in from the car and took from it the letter that Bonnie had given to him. He handed the letter to Rosemary. "What can you tell me about this?"

She removed a pair of wire-rimmed spectacles from the side pocket of her housecoat and glanced briefly at the letter before handing it back. "Nothing."

He handed her another folded sheet of paper—a handwritten recipe written on a sheet of green notepaper with her name and Florida phone number written at the top. She looked at it and scowled.

"Your son gave that to me. He told me you wrote it."

Rosemary looked at him, straight, unflinching, and stubbornly silent.

"You've been writing to my brother's wife."

Rosemary took a deep breath, "Do you mind telling me, Thomas, what this has to do with Morgan family shootings and kidnappings?"

"That's your handwriting, isn't it?"

Rosemary sighed. "Bonnie Bellemare was a former pupil of mine. I liked her, and it pained me to see her deceived."

Tom reached into the knapsack again and removed the defaced photo that Joe found in Herbert Ball's kitchen garbage can. He tried to hand it to Rosemary, but she kept her hands in her lap. He laid the photo on the glass-top table between them. "What can you tell me about this?"

Rosemary bristled, "Once again, Thomas. What has any of this to do with shootings and kidnappings?"

Tom leaned forward. "My mother may have thought that she was the exclusive object of Herbert Ball's attention. But that wasn't true, was it? Mr. Bell visited Florida frequently in the winter months, and not because he had business there."

Rosemary tightened her mouth. "What are you implying?"

"That photo was defaced by someone who was angry with Herbert Bell *and* my mother. There's no evidence of a break-in at Mr. Ball's apartment where that photo was found. Whoever defaced it must have had a key. Do you have a key to Herbert Bell's apartment, Mrs. Ryan?"

Rosemary Ryan closed her eyes and breathed heavily through her nostrils. "I'm only going to ask this one more time, Thomas. What do these very personal questions have to do with your family's unfortunate difficulties?"

Tom reached into his knapsack and retrieved a final piece of paper. "This is a photograph of what remains of the truck that my mother and Herbert Bell were riding in the night they were run off the road and killed. The streaks of paint on the rear bumper and tailgate indicate that it was struck multiple times from behind before going off the road. The color of those streaks matches the color of the Mercedes parked outside this house. The one with the crumpled grill and hood. Your son says that you had an accident."

Rosemary Ryan smiled and scoffed.

"Do you want to elaborate?" asked Tom.

"No. But as it seems you won't go away otherwise, I will tell you this. Yes, I was angry with Herbert and your mother, but not for the reasons you suppose. Herbert Bell was a narcissistic old dandy. But at our age, people make allowances. He was also trying to steal the Coldwater Bank from my son, as you now know.

"I was angry with your mother because she was pressuring a cherished former student to silently suffer the kind of abusive behavior that no woman should have to. Yes, I have a key to Herbert Ball's apartment, and I went there after the tragedy to retrieve some of my things. And yes, I let out my frustrations with both of them on that photograph you found there. But an old woman's anger is not a crime, Thomas, and it's also none of your business!"

Tom lowered his voice and continued quietly, "And the damaged Mercedes parked outside, whose color matches the paint streaks on the back of the truck Herbert Ball was driving when someone angry person ran him off the road and killed him and my mother?"

Rosemary grimaced. "I know nothing about that, Thomas. But unless the store has cleaned it up, you can likely find that same paint on a pair of metal and concrete bumpers at the CVS drive-through pharmacy on Route 6. The dents on the front of the Mercedes should be an exact match."

Tom leaned back and nodded slowly. "Alright. I'll check that out. But you should know that my brother took paint samples from the Mercedes parked out front and the truck that Herbert Bell and my mother were killed in. The lab results comparing the two paint samples should be available shortly."

"Good. Maybe that will put an end to all of this impertinent Morgan nonsense. Now, please let yourself out, Thomas. I've had quite enough of you."

* * *

Unless Rosemary Ryan was a world-class liar, Tom realized that he had come to a dead end. He had figured out who had shot an arrow through his brother's back. The shooter would be getting his just desserts in due course. But as for who killed Herbert and Mary by running Joe's truck off the road, he knew that he was no closer to answering that question than he had been when he first started. Unless the paint samples Joe had taken from the Silverado and the Mercedes came back a match, it seemed likely that the identity of Herbert and Mary's killer would remain a mystery.

The thought of one more conversation with his brother made Tom feel like he had aged twenty years. But there was no avoiding it. He left Wilson Point and drove back to town to have a final Come-To-Jesus session with Joe.

Paulie Grogan was not in his usual spot, doing nothing with his feet propped on MadDog's old desk. The trooper on duty smirked when Tom said he was there to see the Coldwater sheriff, but he led Tom back to the cells without remark. Joe lay where Tom had left him, lying on the slab bunk, staring up at the ceiling. Pulling the now familiar plastic chair next to the bars, Tom began to talk.

Joe might as well have been asleep as Tom summarized his conversations with Andrew and Rosemary Ryan. Nor did he immediately respond when Tom asked him if he'd gotten the results of the car paint analysis. But after a silent and uncomfortable minute, Joe made a snarly, grunting noise, swung his legs off the bunk, and removed a large white envelope from beneath a dirty foam pillow. Then he handed the envelope to Tom and stood back, arms across his chest.

When Tom finished reading, he looked toward the tiny window beyond the cell bars. He could not look at his brother.

"So, what are you going to do now, Boy Scout?"

Chapter Twenty-Four

Joe had once summarized his law enforcement philosophy as "Lock up the dangerous and let God take care of the guilty." In the context of an overworked, small-town sheriff's department, Tom had once been willing to concede that there might be some merit to that philosophy. But Joe had moved far beyond practical adjustment to resource constraint, and he was no longer locking up the dangerous and leaving guilt and punishment to a higher power. Now, *he* was the higher power, prepared to kill either or both. Nothing in the envelope Joe had given him changed that.

So what are you going to do now, Boy Scout?

Oh, hell, Bonnie.

He drove to his brother's house, parked the Buick next to the empty shed, and sat there listening to the click and hum of the cooling car engine while he thought about what he could possibly say or do next. The folder containing the paint analysis lay on the seat beside him. He stared at it for long minutes before climbing slowly from the car and shuffling toward the house.

Bonnie answered his knock and led him through the living room to the back porch, stopping briefly to grab two cups of hot coffee from the kitchen. The kids were at school, and for a while, she and Tom sat in silence, wrapped in blankets, sipping coffee and thinking their own thoughts. Finally, he asked. "What have you told the kids?"

She put down her coffee. "Only what's in the newspapers. And I can hardly believe that. My husband, with a Swiss bank account!"

"That was MadDog's account. Joe may have known about it. But I don't think he ever accessed it or would even have known how."

"I also can't believe that he pled guilty. That's so unlike him."

"He didn't have a choice, Bonnie. It was either that or manslaughter. One of the men he shot was unarmed. Though, in the heat of the moment, I doubt he knew that."

Her voice was bitter. "Mark Tremblay was no kidnapper."

"No. But his cousin was. He made the ransom demand. He shot at Joe and set fire to a cabin with your son and me inside."

Bonnie moved her weight toward the front of her chair. "My head's spinning, Tom. I don't know what to tell the children."

Tom put his hand on hers. "Tell them the truth. That in the heat of a gun battle he didn't start, their dad made a mistake and shot someone he thought was an armed kidnapper. That rather than go to jail for a long time on account of that innocent mistake, he pled guilty to something else—a technical violation of banking laws. That he'll be out in two years. And that in the meantime, Uncle Tommy will stick around to keep everyone in line."

Bonnie stared at him, her mouth half-open. "You're going to stay in Coldwater?"

"Two weeks a month to start. I still have to make a living."

She put her coffee aside, stood, and leaned over to wrap her arms around his shoulders. He allowed the hug, even gently returning it. But his gut ached for what had to come next. "Bonnie..." He handed her the file that Joe had given him.

"What is this?"

"An analysis of paint taken from the back bumper and tailgate of the truck Herbert Ball was driving when he ran off the road, killing him and my mother. Apparently, the truck was hit from behind several times by another vehicle before it ran off the road. That report compares the paint that was left on the wrecked bumper with samples from several other cars."

His sister-in-law's eyes would not meet his.

"Including one parked outside."

Bonnie took a deep breath and gazed somewhere over his head. "Oh, Tom."

He looked at her and waited.

She leaned her weight against the deck rail, her face sad and hard. "I don't know what to say, Tom. Joe's truck, late at night...two people in the front seat...one of them obviously a woman." She turned and looked toward the lake. "I didn't know that my old car *could* push that monster truck off the road, or that there might be a thirty-foot ditch on the other side. Or that it was your mom's boyfriend at the wheel and not my cheating husband."

He stood and put his arm around her shoulder. She turned and looked into his face. "Oh, Tom... Does Joe know?"

"He gave me that report."

"Dear God."

Tom tightened his grip. "Don't worry. He's not going to do anything."

"Oh, Tom. You don't know what he's become."

"I have a good idea. But he's not going to do anything about this. Trust me."

She sat down hard. "What about Paulie Grogan? Does he know? Does anyone else?"

"Only you, me, and Joe have seen that report. And Morgans can keep a secret. We've had practice."

* * *

When Luke came home from school, Tom asked him if he would like to learn how to rattle up a buck. "I want to show you how to find a lost arrow, too, if you're okay to go back to Grandpa Morgan's tree stand." The boy looked away. "You didn't shoot your dad, Luke, if that's what you've been thinking." He put his arm around the boy's shoulders. "I found your arrow stuck in a sugar maple about sixty yards downhill from Grandpa's tree stand. That's the opposite direction from where your dad was shot."

Luke held onto the back of the Adirondack chair and sat down hard.

"Dozens of grown men tramped all over those woods for nearly a week, and not one of them spotted your arrow. Do you know why?" Luke shook his head. "Because they never looked up. If they had, they would have seen it easily—a patch of bright orange fletching against a background of dark hardwoods."

The boy nodded and pulled in a deep breath.

"Deer don't look up either, because their enemies are on the ground, not up in the air. They don't look up unless they sense movement or hear a suspicious noise. That's why bow hunting from a tree stand works."

Luke's eyes found Tom's.

"So what's say you and I climb up to that tree stand where the deer never look, and I'll show you how to rattle up a buck?"

* * *

Tom had been putting off the call to Varné for long enough. He had an idea that might interest *la Sûreté* and salvage the Israeli connection. But if the Frenchman wouldn't pitch it, then it was game over, and there would be no reason for Tom to return to Europe even for two weeks a month. Half expecting to get Varné's voicemail, he was surprised when the Frenchman answered on the first ring. "Tom! *Comment ça va?*"

"That depends, Marc. How would your friends in *la Sûreté* like to get their hands on some state-of-the-art Israeli internet monitoring technology?"

Varné's voice was wary. "I cannot imagine why they would refuse."

"Would you be willing to tell your contact there that you've been talking to an Israeli company about licensing their internet monitoring technology? That if we reach agreement, we would give *la Sûreté* access to everything the Israelis give us. That they'd be able to check it for anything of concern and make any modifications to it they wished. And that we'd commit to use in France only technology that *la Sûreté* has vetted."

There was silence on the other end of the phone. When Varné finally spoke, it was with obvious hesitation. "They might say yes."

"And you? This would only substitute French bugging for Israeli bugging. *La Sûreté* will surely add their own ears to what the Israelis give us."

Varné laughed, "Yes, but they would be French ears. And as I said before, *la Sûreté* is surely listening already."

"Good. And if they say yes? Would you still be reluctant to participate in the film exchange project?"

Varné laughed again. "If *la Sûreté* is in agreement and I have not already shot myself in the feets, I would be happy to accompany you."

Tom breathed a sigh of hope. "Alright. I'm going to give you the number of a Tel Aviv lawyer who can draft the technology license agreement. I'll draft the other agreement and send it to you as soon as I get back to London."

"What is this other agreement, Tom? And what must I do with it?"

"It's a partnership agreement. Read it and sign it. You and I are going to keep a piece of this Israeli technology for ourselves."

* * *

Yvette Huppe called shortly after Tom got off the phone with Varné. Tom was surprised at how lighthearted he felt when he heard her voice. Note to self: When did that last happen?

"Finalment!" she exclaimed. "I have the good news! The German lawyers have done as you suggest."

"Without further negotiation?"

"I am surprised, also. But there is much to do now. The situation with your family, does it permit you to return to Europe?"

"Yes. But I'll need to split my time between here and there for a while."

"Oh." Her voice lost a measure of enthusiasm. "Then we must anticipate the regulatory issues in France, as I advised you."

"We could put operational headquarters in Paris, if that would help."

It was a moment before she answered. "You would be plagued all the time by French bureaucrats, you know."

"Paris has other attractions."

There was another long pause. When Huppe responded, her tone was cautious. "I have had much time to think about your philosophy of values, Thomas. Ours are quite different. They must not, I think, be compatible over the 'long haul.'"

Merde.

"You live much in your head," she continued. "I am not certain that you know how to feel."

What I feel now is deflated.

"You must discover the *joi de vivre,* Thomas. What otherwise is life's purpose?"

Good question. The ultimate question. But surely joy is a result, not a recipe. We're not meant to be lotus-eaters.

"I don't know, Yvette. *Joi de vivre* is an important piece of the human puzzle. In my case, perhaps the missing piece. But I'm at a loss where to look for it."

Once again, there was silence on the end of the phone. Then, in a mock teasing voice, she asked, "May I ask if you are sitting down?"

"What? Yes."

"Good. Because what I would ask will probably shock you. But could you have interest in a different kind of French weekend? Fun and frolic. *Rien de sérieux.*"

"Nothing serious?"

"To begin with, Thomas. You must practice the patience."

It was his turn to pause. Then, with a barely suppressed chuckle, he responded. "I suppose I might rise to the occasion."

* * *

Mrs. Flynn escorted Tom to the library at the back of the rectory. Gauss stepped out from behind his writing desk and gave Tom a gentle hug. "So, you went through with it? If what I read in the Gazette is true."

"It's not. But Rambo is off the streets long enough for him to decide what he wants to be when he grows up. And I've given our friend Jack Thompson something to make sure that the next generation of Morgan men will have to find some other line of work. No more bullies with a badge."

"That will be a welcome change for Coldwater. How do you feel about that?"

"Like a dog who used to chase cars and finally caught one. Now what?"

"And your sister-in-law and her children? How are they holding up?"

"They're a bit shell-shocked. Though the girls haven't gone Goth, and Luke's not setting fire to cats."

Mrs. Flynn appeared at the library door with a tray of coffee and pastries. She placed the tray on a corner of Gauss's trestle table and pressed a hand to Tom's shoulder as she passed. When the priest returned to his chair, Tom took the seat opposite. "How's your German?" he asked.

Gauss looked puzzled at the odd change of subject. "With a surname like mine, it should be better. I've managed to stumble through Meister Eckhart once or twice." Gauss made a vague gesture toward the wall of books. "He's up there somewhere."

Tom took a folder from his messenger bag and handed it to the priest. "Good. Because you're now the holder, in trust, of a 10% interest in a *Europäische Filmbörse GmbH*."

"Never heard of it."

"Few have. It's a German holding company, recently organized to gather data on what people say in internet chat rooms about movies they've seen outside of movie theaters."

"Does this have anything to do with your brother's Swiss bank account troubles?"

"No," Tom laughed. "The Gazette got that part wrong, too."

"So, what does "in trust" mean? And what exactly am I supposed to do with these?" Gauss waived the folder.

"Legally, it means you can't sell any of the shares. Practically, it means that if enough people start to watch movies outside of movie theaters, the trust will have more income than you'll know what to do with. If that happens, I *trust* you to put that money to good use. Build that school on Pocket Island, or whatever else you find that needs doing."

Gauss smiled and at the same time looked serious. "That's very generous of you, Tommy."

"It's a long shot. There's never been much movie viewing outside of theaters. The standard Saturday night date is still dinner and a movie. Not even television killed that. But if movie watching ever changes, *Europäische Filmbörse GmbH* could be worth a lot of money."

Gauss put the folder aside. "Well then, thank you. Now, more importantly, how's your soul?"

Tom laughed again. For some reason, he felt almost giddy. "Upbeat, I'm happy to report."

Gauss poured coffee and slid the tray of pastries across the desk.

"I've made friends with my daimon," Tom explained.

Gauss sat back. "There can't be many who've uttered those words in the last three thousand years. You've got my attention."

"Well, the catalyst was our last conversation. Specifically, the part about "life's purpose," and your admonition that *time's a wastin'*. Your daimon digression got me thinking about all the doors that have opened for me over the years and all the walls I've run into. The challenge to take another look at Plato's theory led me to think that if there is a Platonic 'form' of 'fulfilled human', then by definition it includes a number of variations. "Life's purpose" may not be binary. Not X or Y, either/or. All of us go through periodic changes. Perhaps discontent isn't a sign that what we've been doing has been wrong. Maybe it's just a sign that it's time to move on. Like a crustacean outgrowing its shell. Time to find a bigger one."

Gauss put down his cup and folded his hands on the desk. "So where does Tommy Morgan think he might go looking for this new shell, or whatever it is?"

Tom spread his hands. "I don't know. But you were right: 'You break it, you bought it.' I'll stay in Coldwater until things settle down. Then I'll split my time between here and Europe until my brother gets out of Auburn."

Gauss nodded. "Do you have any idea of what this new *shell* might look like?"

Tom shook his head. "Not a clue. I suppose I'll just have to keep my eye open for a sign. Doors and walls, as the case may be."

Gauss smiled. "Some might call that prayer. I hear it works."

Acknowledgements

One of the many wonderful things about having grandchildren is that they can provide an uncritical audience for spontaneous story telling. I would be remiss if I didn't thank Jack, Lillian, Annie, Henry, Mabel, Sam, Arthur and Nora for their incomprehensible appetite for Papa Jim's nonsensical stories. He would not be the bard he aspires to be without you.

About the Author

James A. Ross has at various times been a Peace Corps volunteer in the Congo, a Congressional staffer, and a Wall Street lawyer. His historical novel, *Hunting Teddy Roosevelt*, and his Coldwater mystery series have won numerous literary awards in their respective genres. Ross is a frequent contributor to, and several times winner of, the live storytelling competition, Cabin Fever Story Slam. He has also appeared as a guest storyteller on the Moth Main Stage and other venues. His live performances, online stories and more can be found on his website: jamesrossauthor.com

AUTHOR WEBSITE:
https://jamesrossauthor.com

SOCIAL MEDIA HANDLES:
FB: https://www.facebook.com/james.a.ross.author
Twitter: https://www.facebook.com/JamesARoss10
Instagram: @jamesrossauthor

Also by James A. Ross

Hunting Teddy Roosevelt

Coldwater Revenge

Coldwater Endgame

Printed in the USA
CPSIA information can be obtained
at www.ICGtesting.com
LVHW091535221024
794497LV00002B/231

9 781685 126742